CHAPTER ONE

Greer

*C*av lied to me.

About everything.

Bile rises in my throat. *How could I be so wrong?*

I wrap my arms around my body, cold chills racing across my skin despite the heat of the Belizean morning. Static fills my head. Or is that the blood rushing in my ears?

My brother's voice pierces the white noise. "He's my fucking half brother."

That can't be right. Impossible.

I'm transported back to the day Creighton told me all the secrets our uncle had spewed. That Creighton wasn't his nephew. Which meant he wasn't my full brother. That our mother was the mistress of some mobster who would never marry her because he was already married.

And Cav is the mobster's son too.

Every piece I fit together in my brain triggers another twist of my belly until I'm nauseated.

But one thought overarches it all, and I curl my fingers into the fabric of my shirt to keep my hands from visibly trembling as I repeat it in my head. *Cav lied to me. Every step of the way.*

I know I should look at him, but I can't do it. I'm not physically equipped to face that kind of deceit head-on. My eyes won't cooperate, studying the lines of grout on the tile floor instead.

Another shiver rips through me, and this time I almost throw up in my mouth.

Please, God, tell me I didn't accidentally commit some kind of incest.

"Who is your mother?" I ask Cav, my voice shaking as I stare at the floor.

"Greer, look at me." His tone is quiet but forceful.

"Don't fucking tell her what to do," Creighton says, the words firing like invisible bullets at Cav.

"Because only you get to tell her what to do?" Cav's voice is laced with acid. "You have to control everyone and everything around you, Karas. She's a fucking person with a mind of her own. Not one of your subordinates."

The front door to the house flies open, but I don't honestly care who else is coming in. All I want is the answer to my question and for the buzzing in my head to stop, preferably thanks to lots and lots of alcohol. I think I've earned it.

"Who is your mother?" I repeat, perilously close to

ABOUT THIS BOOK

Greer Karas has been mine since the first day I saw her.

I walked away because she deserved better than I could offer, but I always planned to come back and stake my claim when the time was right.

But true to form, Greer wasn't willing to wait. She threw down a challenge, and I'm meeting her head-on.

I'm not walking away this time, because sometimes you have to fight dirty for love.

DIRTY
LOVE

Book Two of the The Dirty Girl Duet

Meghan March

Editor: Pam Berehulke, Bulletproof Editing
www.bulletproofediting.com

Cover design: @ By Hang Le
www.byhangle.com

Photo: @ Darren Birks Photography
www.darrenbirksphotography.com

Interior Design: Stacey Blake, Champagne Formats
www.champagneformats.com

Visit my website at www.meghanmarch.com.

ISBN: 978-1-943796-85-4

hysteria.

It isn't Cav who answers me, though. Creighton does.

"She was Dom Casso's mistress after our mother, Greer. You're not related to this piece of shit. Only I am."

If the logical part of my brain were functioning correctly, I probably would have pieced that together myself without needing to ask, but I'm too off-balance right now. Something inside me feels broken, but I refuse to admit it's my heart.

It can't be.

"Greer—" Cav starts again, but Cannon interrupts.

"Crey, you ready? The airport isn't going to let the jet sit for much longer. They want us out now." My brother's second-in-command—his sidekick, really—steps through the door to the bedroom.

"Come on, let's go," Creighton says to me, holding out his hand.

"Greer, you're not leaving with him. Look at me, goddammit." Cav's tone is pure command, but I don't make any move to comply.

"Don't you fucking tell her what to do." Creighton's words resemble a growl.

White noise overwhelms my thoughts. Information and emotion overload. I'm paralyzed, my feet rooted to the floor, my arms frozen around me.

"Look at me, baby girl. Please."

I drag my gaze from the floor at Cav's feet and up toward his face. It could have taken five seconds or five minutes, but my sense of time is shattered. Twenty minutes ago, I was asleep with this man wrapped around me, but when I look at him now, I see a stranger.

I don't know him. At all. I never have. The truth beats into my head like the waves crashing on the shore outside.

Creighton steps closer and wraps a strong arm around my shoulders, allowing me to sag into his strength. My big brother has never done anything but shield me from everything bad in the world. He's the one person in my life I can truly count on. No hidden motives. Just . . . overbearing protectiveness.

"We're leaving. And if you so much as come within two hundred yards of her, I'll have Dom deal with you."

Cav's father. The mobster. Creighton's father. The mobster.

I can't. Can't process. The pieces aren't snapping together anymore; they're lying scattered on the metaphorical floor of my brain like a toddler threw a tantrum.

When Creighton's feet move and the arm around me forces me to step toward the door, I go.

"She's not leaving with you."

It's a declaration, but I can barely hear it over the buzzing in my head.

Cannon swoops in behind me, and I imagine he and Cav are facing off like boxers in a ring. I don't turn my head to see. My body won't have it.

He lied. About everything. The words tumble through my brain on repeat. I gave him the most vulnerable parts of me, and he's never given me the truth. About anything.

Every repetition is another fist to the gut. And if I'm being honest—maybe to my heart.

The static grows louder in my head, drowning out the

shouting in the bedroom as I let Creighton lead me, one foot in front of the other, out the door of the beach house.

So much for fantasies becoming real.

CHAPTER TWO

Cav

"Get out of my fucking way." If this slick fuck doesn't step back right now, I'm going to knock his head off his shoulders. Greer just walked out the door, looking half-drunk from the bullshit she was fed.

I need to get to her. Need to explain. It wasn't all a lie. She's only getting half the story—the half they want her to hear—and now this prick is blocking my path from the bedroom.

I don't hesitate to swing. What shocks me is how quickly he dodges the blow—like a seasoned boxer. What surprises me even more is the fist that flies toward my jaw and connects.

The burst of pain doesn't register because everything is already black.

CHAPTER THREE

Greer

Cav didn't even try to follow me.

It's just one more thought that joins those on shuffle in my brain as we reach cruising altitude and the jet's Wi-Fi kicks in. The static has died down, and now I feel . . . empty. Hurt. And the hurt is filling in the emptiness faster than I expected.

After digging into the bag of clothes Creighton stashed in the bedroom at the back of the jet, I change out of the dress I wore last night. The dress I wore before I gave up that last slip of my virginity . . . to a man who lied to me from the day we met.

Great judgment, Greer.

I mentally apologize to the anonymous owner of the dress as I stuff it into the tiny garbage can of the jet's bathroom. I wish I could shed all of the hurt so easily. But no, there's only one solution for that—alcohol.

I push open the door from the private bedroom to the main cabin where Creighton and Cannon are seated across from each other in wide tan leather seats. Each of Creighton's jets seems to be nicer than the last, but I'm not in the mood to appreciate the well-appointed interior with its rich leather, dark wood, and brushed silver accents. No, I'm in the mood to appreciate the liquor cabinet.

Both men watch me as I walk directly to it. I ignore Cannon's question about whether I need anything.

The only thing I need is in my hand. A fifth of Grey Goose. I don't even need a glass. On a whim, I grab a can of cranberry juice to chase it with, not to mix.

"Is that really a good idea?" Creighton asks, his tone surprisingly condescension-free.

"It's the only idea I have right now. Drinking until I pass out and forget the last couple of weeks sounds perfect."

Creighton doesn't object.

"I grabbed your purse too, on the way out," Cannon says, jerking his head toward where my bag sits tucked under a seat.

With my free fingers, I snag that too. "Awesome."

I lock myself back into the cabin and turn on my phone. After it didn't work the first few days in Belize, I decided to free myself from constantly checking it and decided to enjoy being disconnected by turning it off. My battery is still at sixty-seven percent, which is plenty for my next task.

The Wi-Fi signal is strong as I log on to my Skype account. Unannounced Skype calls are the devil's work; you just don't do that to a girl. But Banner will have to forgive me because this is a serious situation. I don't know what time zone I'm in, but I decide to risk it anyway by tapping on her name.

Moments later, my best friend's face fills the screen. "Where the hell have you been? And if I weren't so damn worried about you, I would've made you call back in five minutes when I didn't look like a survivor of the zombie apocalypse."

Banner's hair is wild, sticking out in all directions. Eye makeup that must not have come off completely last night is smudged under her lower lashes. I don't even know what day it is.

"Did I wake you?"

"Nah, I'm laying here wishing I could quit my job and run away with the circus. I hear those strongmen can deliver quite the pounding."

Against all odds, a laugh bubbles up inside me. This is exactly what I need—my best friend and some booze.

I situate my phone against the stack of pillows on the bed and hold up the bottle of vodka in front of the screen.

"It's five o'clock somewhere, right?" My voice is faux cheerful, and tears gather at the corners of my eyes.

Banner doesn't miss a thing. She shoves up in bed and shakes her finger at the camera.

"If he so much as hurt one hair on your head—or anywhere else you inadvisably have hair—I'm gonna kill him."

I shake my head. "I don't want to talk about it. I want to get hammered and I need my best friend. We gotta go shot for shot or I'm never going to get enough down to forget this."

Banner's face crumples. "It was that bad?"

I nod.

"I'm sorry, babe. Let me get my supplies and I'll be right back. Don't go anywhere."

The picture on my screen bounces as Banner carries the phone with her to the kitchen. Her bright red silk nightgown obscures the picture until she sets the phone up against something on her kitchen table.

"One more sec. Gotta get the good stuff."

She's back in moments with a matching bottle of vodka and a shot glass. "Okay. I'm not saying I'm not gonna puke, but after last night, I can use a little hair of the dog."

Something occurs to me. "Do you need to go to work?"

She shakes her head. "Nope, going to e-mail them to tell them Fernando the Brazilian Strongman and I are running away to Rio where he's going to keep me so well fucked, I won't be able to walk, let alone work."

I tilt my head and study her face. With a choking laugh, I say, "You really did go to the circus, didn't you? Oh my God, you fucked a carny?"

Banner's eyes dart sideways, telling me she was lying about "hearing" that strongmen can deliver a good pounding. "I got sick of the techie guys at work. I needed a man with arms bigger than mine. Preferably bigger than my thighs. I'm not apologizing for my walk on the carny side. It was awesome. The all-you-can-eat elephant ears were a bonus."

I cover my face with both hands and peek through my

fingers. "Oh my God. Where the hell did you find a circus in Manhattan?"

This time her gaze darts to the floor and her cheeks flush.

"Banner?" I drop my hands and pin her with my best *tell me right now* look.

Her voice is a mumble when she next speaks. "Jersey."

Of course.

"And why aren't you still in the strongman's bed?"

I need to hear more. Preferably the whole story, because at least Banner's life is more ridiculous than mine, and it has a shot at distracting me from everything I want to forget.

She coughs and speaks into her hand. "What was that?" Lowering her hand, she admits, "They had to pack up and drive to Pennsylvania. No more strong cock for this girl. It's heartbreaking, really. Fernando was amazing. I didn't understand a single word he said because my Portuguese is nonexistent, but who needs words when you've got an eleven-inch cock with the girth of jumbo summer sausage? My pussy may never be the same again . . . but at least I'll have the memories."

She finishes on a wistful note, and I'm so damn glad that my best friend is absolutely nuts.

"I love you, B."

"Love you too, girl. Now, uncap that bottle and let's get day drunk."

I twist off the top and lift the bottle to my lips and chug. The vodka slides down my throat in a cool rush. Smooth. Silky. Deliciously mind-numbing.

Best. Idea. Ever.

Banner regales me with stories of the strongman, and I work on blocking out every memory involving Cav. She doesn't ask for details because she's that kind of friend. The kind that knows instinctively that I wouldn't be swilling vodka like it's water while sitting in the back of my brother's private jet unless something had gone sideways in the worst way possible.

Or at least, I thought she took the hint that I didn't want to talk about it. But no, my sneaky best friend decides to wait until I'm five shots in and my capacity for lying is nil.

"So, what the hell happened? You were here and the gossip rags slapped the label of Cav Westman's hot new girlfriend on you, and then you freaking disappeared. I about lost my mind worrying. I stormed your brother's office, and Cannon told me you were safe but laying low, and escorted me out of the building. Nothing else. I've been waiting impatiently for you to call, and now you call and want to get wasted. You gotta tell me what's going on, woman."

"Can we shelve this conversation for later?"

"Nope." Banner pops the *p*. "Spill."

I take a deep breath and give it all to her in one fell swoop. "Cannon shoved us in a plane and sent us to some tiny island off the coast of Belize where we fucked and ate and laid in the sun for the last however many days until Creighton showed up to drop the bomb that Cav . . ." I pause because I haven't shared the mob connection with Banner, and I doubt Creighton would want me to. Quick thinking has me changing my words to something vaguer. "Well, he's been lying to me since the beginning. About everything."

Holding up a finger, Banner grabs the neck of the bottle of vodka and pours another shot. "Get ready to chug, girlie, because that deserves more liquor."

I lift my bottle in a toast and pour more cool vodka down my throat. One shot, two shots . . . maybe more. Who knows at this point? All I know is that the bottle isn't empty yet, and I'm still conscious.

When Banner slams her shot glass on her table, she crosses her arms in front of her and adopts a serious expression.

"So he broke your heart . . . but did he break your ass?"

Thank God I've finished swallowing because I would have spewed vodka all over this silky duvet and the screen of my phone.

"Jesus, B. Really?" I open my mouth to protest that he didn't break anything, but she keeps going.

"It's an important question. And I'm already getting drunk and it's not even ten a.m., and therefore I deserve an answer. Are you still a back-door virgin?"

Glaring at her through the Skype connection, I flatten my lips before I burst into drunken giggles. "I can still feel the twinge in my ass, if you really want to know the truth."

Banner's eyes get huge. "No. Way. You did it! My little girl has finally grown up and taken a cock where no cock has ever gone before! This deserves to be tweeted. We must memorialize it on the interwebs."

Grabbing up her iPad, she types furiously.

"Uh, no way in hell are you tweeting that. It's my news."

I know I'm making a huge mistake as soon as I reach for my phone and minimize the Skype app in favor of Twitter. And yet I don't care. It's probably the vodka fueling this poor decision making. And I mean probably as in *definitely*.

"I'm not saying anything about my ass, but the world should know that having a big cock just means the guy is an even bigger dick."

Pulling up the infamous @GreerOneBadBitchKaras Twitter account that helped my ad go viral, I compose a masterpiece of a tweet. A Twitter-piece, I decide to call it.

I mumble to Banner as I tap out my 140 characters of awesomeness. *Damn, vodka makes me just as creative as tequila.*

Size doesn't matter if it just means you're an even bigger dickhead. #BigDick #KissMyAss #NeverAgain #GreerOut #NoCavDo #FuckUVeryMuch

Reading it out loud to Banner takes three tries because I can't stop laughing. And if there are tears sneaking out of the corners of my eyes, they're totally from the laughter. I refuse to admit anything else.

"Do it!"

I hit TWEET before I can second-guess myself or attempt more creative hashtags.

My notifications blow up within seconds. *Whoa.* Apparently, ever since I hooked up with Cav and the press started linking our names, my Twitter following has really grown.

I check out my profile, taking a second to give a nod of approval to the picture Banner chose when she helped me set it up. Followers: 1.2 million.

Uh-oh. A niggle of doubt creeps through the vodka-driven safety cocooning me. The retweets and likes climb in number.

"Uh, Banner. Did you know I have 1.2 million Twitter followers?"

Her eyes round hysterically. "Say what now?"

"One point two million," I say, repeating the words very, very slowly.

"Holy shitballs. Cav's going to get the message, that's for damn sure."

The lock turns, and the door to the bedroom flies open and slams against the wall. I spin around to face the door, leaving my phone propped up on the pillow.

Creighton, my dear brother, is wearing an expression that would not only frighten small children, but armies of small countries.

Oops.

He holds up a phone, its screen facing me. "What the fuck are you thinking? Cannon and my PR team follow this asinine account on Twitter, and in the last two minutes we've gotten four calls between us that you've decided to exercise poor judgment. So again, I ask, *what the fuck are you thinking*, Greer?"

Searching my liquor-soaked brain for any kind of explanation, I lift the bottle instead. "This is good vodka."

Creighton's expression turns even more thunderous. He reaches out and yanks the bottle from my hand. "Enough."

From far away, I hear Banner's voice.

"Whoa, big brother. Don't get your boxers in a twist. Wait, do you wear boxers? Briefs? What about that side-kick of yours? His are always shoved straight up his tightly clenched ass cheeks. You might want to round up an underwear-retrieval operation for him. It's probably damaging to his health, and most definitely damaging to his scrotum. *Scrotum.* What a weird word."

I'm too drunk to cringe at my best friend's priceless monologue. Instead, I grab my phone off the pillow and point to the screen. "She has a valid point."

"Hang up now. Delete the tweet. No more booze."

Turning the screen back to face me, I wave at Banner. "I think the party just ended. I'll fill you in later."

"Okay, hope your ass feels better. Maybe you need a medium-sized cock next time. You can't give up on anal yet!"

This time, I do cringe. That's something my brother never needed to hear.

"'Bye." I wave again and tap the screen to disconnect before looking up at Creighton sheepishly. "Can you maybe pretend you didn't hear that—"

"Already bleached from my memory. We're never discussing it again. Now, delete the damn tweet."

Cannon's voice comes from the main cabin. "It's already been retweeted over seven thousand times. Can't put this cat back in the bag, but you need to delete it anyway."

"Seven thousand times?" *Shit. Bad Greer. Bad vodka.*

"Motherfucker. Jesus, Greer. You know how to get people's attention. Now, come on. I can't trust you alone anymore." He snatches the phone from my hand and wraps his fingers around my wrist to pull me off the bed.

As I follow him out into the main cabin, he tosses my phone to Cannon. "Delete it. Do whatever damage control you can. Fuck, shut down the goddamn Twitter account."

I open my mouth to protest, but snap it shut when both men look at me like I'm a particularly troublesome child. Which I suppose I kinda am. *I suck.*

And I'm hammered. Instead of sinking into one of the leather chairs, I lie down on the couch and reach underneath for the blanket that's always stowed there in these jets.

When I'm covered, I mumble, "Wake me up when we get home."

Sleep has almost claimed me when Creighton says, "Oh, Greer. You're not going home."

CHAPTER
FOUR

Cav

Motherfucking bastard. I move my jaw from side to side, making sure that piece of shit Cannon Grove didn't break it. It clicks just like it always has, but god-dammit, it hurts like a motherfucker. Cheap shot. I wasn't expecting him to swing rather than threaten.

My mistake, and it won't happen again.

It's not like I have a glass jaw, either. That prick hit really damn hard. Harder than I ever would have expected coming from a guy wearing a suit in the tropics. Valuable lesson, I guess. Don't judge a guy's punch based on his clothes. The next time I get a shot at him, though, I'll take it. He deserves it.

I've already searched the house. Every single room. Greer is gone. Her purse and phone are gone too.

Watching her lean against her brother after he delivered the news isn't something I ever want to repeat. Greer is a strong woman, and guilt lashes at me for being the reason she crumpled.

Fuck. After these last several days, I felt like we were building a new, more solid level of trust between us. But how solid can something be when you build it on a foundation of lies? If I'm being honest with myself, I knew this was all going to come crashing down sooner rather than later. But that doesn't mean I have to accept it for what it is.

There's a knock on the bedroom door.

"Come in."

"Mr. Westman, would you like lunch while you wait for your plane?"

Cannon told Juan and Rea that I had to be out of the house as soon as my own jet arrived. Too bad the joke was on them. My jet subscription means that flights on short notice, especially international flights, can't always be accommodated. The call I made today confirmed that fact.

"I'm staying until tomorrow, Juan. Jet should be here by nine a.m., and I'll be out of your hair as soon as I can."

"Okay, sir. I'll notify the owners when the house will be vacated, and Mr. Karas as well."

As much as I hate Karas being kept up-to-date on my movements, I don't have much choice. At least this gives me the rest of the day to regroup. Notifications on my phone are piling up—something my publicist and her assistant usually handle. But today they're constant.

I click on my Twitter app to find out what the hell is going on.

Having high numbers of notifications isn't out of the

ordinary these days because everyone seems to have an opinion they want to tweet and mention me in, but rarely do I read them or respond. I'm about to change my mind when I see the first tweet I'm mentioned in.

> *Trouble in paradise per the creative @ GreerOneBadBitchKaras. But at least we know @ TheRealCavWestman has a big cock. #CelebGossip #Breakups*

What the fuck? It's the breakups hashtag that pisses me off. Greer and I aren't done. Not by a long shot. I click on Greer's Twitter handle and see what she wrote.

Oh, Greer. That naughty, naughty girl. When I track her down, she isn't going to sit for a week without feeling the sting of my hand on her ass. If she thinks this is the end, she's in for a rude awakening.

What she doesn't realize is I already know how big a mistake I made when I walked away from her three years ago, and I'm not going to do it again.

CHAPTER FIVE

Greer

A hand shaking my shoulder wakes me up, and I blink at the harsh light of the interior of the jet. "Wanna sleep."

"You can sleep when we get where we're going."

Groaning, I force myself into a sitting position and immediately regret the decision. My stomach flops violently, and I lunge for the door to the bedroom and the connecting lavatory.

Note to self: *Don't ever puke in a jet again. Ewww.*

Creighton waits at the door with a bottle of water and a stack of napkins. "You going to be okay?"

Grabbing both the napkins and the water, I attempt to hide my misery—and shame. I'm a complete and total fuckup.

"I just want my bed."

Creighton's expression shifts into something unreadable. "I'm afraid that's not possible."

"What?" I choke out after swallowing down a gulp of water.

"I couldn't take you back to New York. The paparazzi are going to eat you alive after your little Twitter stunt."

So I'm being stashed somewhere again. "Where are we?" My brain flips through the possibilities. "Nashville?"

Creighton shakes his head. "No. There are way too many paparazzi in Nashville these days. But you're close."

I come up blank. I don't know any other places in Tennessee.

"Where?"

"Kentucky."

Kentucky? It might as well be another foreign country for as familiar as I am with it.

"Why?"

"Because we've kept up Holly's grandma's house and it's vacant. No one is going to come looking for you here unless you blast out your location to the press." His expression hardens when he adds, "Which you better not do."

"I'm sorry, I—"

"Didn't think before you acted. I'm getting that loud and clear. I've also watched stock prices fall by three percent in the last two hours." Creighton crosses his arms over his chest. "You're an adult. A professional. When are you going to realize that your actions have consequences? Your money is at stake here too, Greer. You're losing millions with every stunt you pull."

"I'm not trying to pull stunts—"

"And yet you are. I don't know what the hell happened to the sister who was worried more about her job than her social media accounts, but when you find her, let her know I'm waiting for her to make an appearance."

It's a low blow, and Creighton knows it.

"Maybe I decided it was time to start living? Maybe I realized that work isn't the only thing I have to look forward to in life."

"Then fucking act like a responsible adult. I have a pregnant wife and a multi-billion-dollar empire to run, and I can't keep chasing after you to clean up your messes."

Ouch. Another direct hit.

"Look, I'm sorry. This . . . hasn't been the most normal time in my life. Everything shifted and I can't keep a grip on it."

"Then how about you lay off the booze while you're plotting world domination with Banner. That'd be a start."

I nod. I have nothing further to say because he's right. I've fucked up royally, and I have no explanation for my actions other than emotional terrorism and alcohol.

"I'm sorry."

"Come here." Creighton pulls me in close and hugs me hard. "You're my baby sister, and I want nothing but the best for you. We're going to clean this up, and then we'll find you some decent guy who isn't going to cheat on you or lie to you. Maybe even someone you can build a life with. I know you're looking for the same thing I was, Greer. Our childhood was fucked. Our sense of family was completely screwed up. But when you find the right person, that shit all fades away and the future becomes a hell of a lot brighter."

The idea of my brother finding me a guy straight up terrifies me, but I decide to keep my own counsel on this one. Besides, I don't want to talk this close to his face because I just puked up a lot of vodka.

"Thank you," I say instead, aiming my words at his chest. "Consider the stunts done, especially if you can get me to a bed where I can pass out for the rest of my natural-born life."

Creighton squeezes me tighter before releasing me.

"You got it."

Holly's gran's house is cute and welcoming, but I don't spend much time poking around before I head up the creaking stairs and spot the bed Creighton directed me to. I climb under the covers fully clothed and force my brain to quiet. I just want sleep and to forget this entire day.

It can't be real. None of it can be real.

CHAPTER SIX

Cav

"What the fuck do you mean, she's not here?" My voice is low, humming with rage. I'm fresh off the jet and determined to find Greer and set things straight.

From the way his face pales, I'm scaring the shit out of the doorman, and I couldn't care less.

"I mean that Ms. Karas hasn't been in the building in several days. I'm under orders to keep collecting her mail and locking it up until further notice."

Where the hell could she have gone? Or, the better question is—where the hell did her big brother stash her this time? To find an answer to that, I have to dig deeper than this doorman. I have more resources at my disposal than Creighton Karas gives me credit for, and it won't take me long to find her.

I walk out of the building, heading for my past.

Dominic Casso holds court in the same building now as he did when I was a kid. Ma would take me there sometimes when she was dropping stuff off.

Everyone knew she was the mistress and I was the bastard son. Why the man couldn't manage to produce a kid with his wife, I have no idea, but my suspicion is he didn't spend enough time in her bed to get the job done. As far as I know, I have at least one half sister and maybe another half brother, but Dom has never confirmed or denied it. Probably because I never asked and I don't plan to.

The small brownstone sits on the edge of Hell's Kitchen, and I'm surprised he's never upgraded. Then again, Dom didn't get to his current position by being flashy or stupid. No, he's calculating and ruthless. Information doesn't flow from him unless he wants it to, and anyone who steps out of line is knocked back with the force of his will—or the back of his hand.

I've often been on the receiving end, and one time in particular stands out clearly in my memory . . .

"You had one job. One fucking job." Dom's tone was quietly menacing. "Watch her. Protect her. Never let her know you fucking exist."

His fist slammed down on the desk, and the bronze

paperweight in the shape of an apple-sized globe jumps with the force. He killed a man with that paperweight once. In front of me. I was fifteen, just being brought into the family business. Dom had decreed it was time for me to earn my keep and stop living on the money he paid my ma.

"But you couldn't even do that. You just had to cross the goddamned line." He grabbed the paperweight off the old wooden desk and tossed it back and forth between his hands.

Would he lob it at my head? My boxing lessons from Franco gave me good odds that I could duck quick enough, but I didn't want to bet on them.

"No explanation?" He scowled at me. "You've got nothing to say for yourself?"

I never let my expression change during his tirade. Nothing I could say would change what I'd done . . . disobeyed the king.

"Open your fucking mouth, Cavanaugh, and say something. Did you fuck the girl?"

Now he was edging closer to my personal line. He might be the king, but I wouldn't let him say a damned word against Greer. I'd snatch that paperweight out of the air and hurl it back at him before he realized what was happening.

"Watch what you say about her."

Dom reared back in his seat as if shoved by the vehemence in my tone. "What did you say to me?" Rarely had I ever talked back to him, and his shock was clear.

"I said, watch what you say about her. She's a lady. She

deserves your respect." I expected my low words to yield threats of violence, not a look of approval. But my relief lasted only a moment.

"Glad you understand that she's out of your league, boy. You've got no business letting her know you exist, let alone pretending to be part of her world. You're the fucking maintenance man and she's an heiress."

He wasn't telling me anything I didn't already know. Greer was too good for me. If she didn't have a problem with it, why should I?

"She doesn't seem to mind."

Dom slammed his fist on the desk again. "Well, I fucking mind, and when I tell one of my men to take on a job, I expect him to do that job exactly the way I say. You do not overstep the line, boy. That's a good way to lose your place and your life."

So, what did I do? I was being warned off Greer, and yet I wasn't ready to be done with her. I'd known from the beginning that crossing the line was a bad idea, but she drew me in. She was still drawing me in.

I waited for Dom to demand that I agree to stay away from her, but in his arrogance, he assumed his words were all that were necessary. He was wrong.

"Now, get the hell out of my office and back to work. I don't need to be dealing with your shit. I'm too fucking busy for pissant shit."

I turned to leave the office, but his voice stopped me at the door.

"Cav, hear me now. You fuck up again and you're gone. Done. Out. So don't fuck up."

It wasn't the first time and wouldn't be the last time I was called to the carpet in front of Dom Casso's wide wooden desk with the globe paperweight. But today, I'm not yanking open the door because he summoned me. No, I'm here demanding answers.

Two men draw their pieces on me when the door swings wide.

"You trying to get shot, kid?"

Dom stands behind his desk, both hands pressed to the leather blotter. The damn paperweight is still there, and I can't help but wonder how many people have died due to blunt force trauma with a little help from the world.

"I'm here for answers."

Dom's gaze narrows on me, his dark eyebrows, much like my own, drawing together.

"Must be something special if it's making you ballsy enough to come here demanding things from me."

"Greer Karas. Where is she? And when the hell did you tell Creighton Karas you were his father?"

Dom lowers himself into the chair, leans back, and crosses his arms. His dark eyes, nothing like mine, thank God, never leave my face.

"It's been fucking years, and you still don't know how to leave that girl alone."

"I don't take orders from you anymore."

"And yet you're here asking for my help."

Impasse. Because I won't beg for that help. I have other ways to learn what I need to know, but this should have

29

been the quickest way to get all the answers I'm looking for today.

"When did you spill to Karas? And why?"

"You're not part of the family anymore, Cav. What makes you think I should share a damn thing with you?"

To hear my father tell me I wasn't part of the only family I ever had should hurt, and maybe it would if I hadn't been immune to his barbs since I was a kid.

"She's my woman. I'm keeping her. So I might not be part of the Casso family, according to you, but I'm going to be part of the Karas family. Just wait."

"Karas will never let it happen. He'll do everything he can to keep her from you."

"He can't hide her forever."

"He will when he learns the rest of the truth."

My entire body stiffens in shock. "He doesn't know already?"

Dom shakes his head slowly from side to side, one corner of his mouth curving in a way that is more malicious than friendly.

"No, but he can learn the rest of the story anytime I want him to. So think long and hard about whether you want to push me, son."

He says *son* to bait me, but Dom doesn't realize I'm beyond caring about my paternity. I refuse to allow his threats to sway me from tracking down Greer. Either way, it's clear I'm not getting any help here.

"That's what I thought," Dom says, triumph edging his tone. "Now, get your ass out of my city and back to Hollywood where you belong with all those other California nuts. Don't come back to New York."

He hasn't even answered the question I asked about Karas, which makes this visit even more pointless.

"I'll leave New York when I'm damn good and ready. And I'll stay out of your way, if you stay out of mine."

Without waiting for a response, I turn and head for the door, knocking my shoulder into one of his henchmen on the way out.

Next stop, the best friend.

CHAPTER SEVEN

Greer

Sunlight streams through the window and I roll over in bed, seeking the warmth of the man beside me. The heat isn't there.

Is Cav already up? My eyes still closed, I reach out—and feel nothing but the soft bumps of a quilt. Reality invades like a bitch slap to the face, and my eyes snap open.

The sunlight streaming in through the window isn't the blindingly beautiful Belizean sun. No, it's . . . *Where the hell am I again?* My head aches and my mouth tastes like days-old caviar. *Blech.* For the record, I hate caviar.

I take in my surroundings while moving as little as possible. Delicate white wooden furniture, lilac wallpaper, and lace curtains. The room of a girl, not an adult.

Right. Kentucky. Creighton stashed the sister who can't keep her shit together in Holly's gran's house in the backwoods.

Noises come from the kitchen below, along with the scent of bacon. *Creighton? Cav?* No, not Cav. Because that son of a bitch lied to me from the beginning.

Squeezing my eyes closed against the prick of tears, I can see his face right before Creighton stormed in on our little haven. *Determination. Sadness.* Guilt.

"I love you. You're mine. And not even Creighton Fucking Karas is going to keep us apart."

Sorry, Cav. That's where you're wrong.

Everything else that happened after is a blur courtesy of my screwed-up emotions and vodka.

Lately, I've become all too familiar with the state of *hungover as hell.* Do I have a problem? I don't even know if I'm in denial because I've never thought about it. Clue number one that I should back off on the *booze solves all ills* school of problem-solving is how crappy I feel right now.

And then I remember the Twitter stunt.

Shit.

Did I delete it?

Searching the surface of the small nightstand next to the bed, I come up empty when I look for my phone. *Oh crap.* Did I lose it?

More noise comes from downstairs, and I decide that even with the pounding headache and questionable stomach, I need to get my ass out of bed and downstairs to find out what the plan is and when I can actually go home. I know I'm going to face another lecture about drinking and tweeting, but I can face that as long as the reward is breakfast.

A small bag Creighton liberated from my apartment rests on top of a desk, and I grab the necessities and make my way into the small connecting bathroom.

Fifteen minutes later, I'm showered, dressed, and making my way downstairs.

"Thought you'd sleep forever when you didn't rush down here at the smell of bacon," a familiar voice calls out before I reach the kitchen.

Cannon has been part of my life since Creighton's business really took off. They were friends before that, but apparently not the kind you introduce your little sister to. I had a mad crush on him when I was younger, but it didn't take long for him to become another annoying older brother who liked to tell me what to do and spoil my fun. My crush died hard and fast.

"I was out, I guess. Where's Crey?"

I lower myself into a chair, attempting not to jar my head too much. I scavenged some ibuprofen from the medicine cabinet upstairs, but considering it expired four years ago, I'm not holding my breath that it's going to work any miracles.

Cannon slides a plate in front of me—scrambled eggs and bacon. Nothing fancy, but then again, he's no gourmet chef. Actually, I think he employs a chef.

"Thank you."

He doesn't answer my question about my brother until he sits down across from me at the wooden table that takes up the center of the small kitchen.

"Crey headed back to Nashville. He didn't want to be

away from Holly any longer than he had to be. Actually, I'm shocked he didn't let me go after you without him, because he hasn't been leaving her side for anything lately."

Guilt settles in my sour stomach, and the appeal of the food in front of me falls several notches. Silence hangs between us for long moments until the sound of a toaster popping interrupts.

"Maybe toast is a better idea for you."

Cannon stands again, and I let my gaze follow him as he butters the white bread toast and drops two slices of it on my plate.

How long has it been since I had white bread? A million years? My aunt served the kind of bread you could kill someone with if you swung it hard enough at his head. Basically, the consistency of a paperweight—but packed with healthy benefits.

I reach for the toast and crunch into it, finding that I'm not as hungover as the last time I got hammered and did something completely idiotic. I thought I was so smart for getting Cav's attention again with that ad. Look at how much good that did me.

I refuse to admit my heart is well and truly cracked by the lies he fed me. Maybe not even so much by the lies as the fact that he made me believe in us. Believe we had a future. All that pretending we were real and we could have a life together set me up for a crushing fall when the truth came out.

Looking at Cannon over my toast, I decide to dig for more answers. With the exception of Creighton, Cannon always knows more about any given situation than everyone else combined.

"How did you and Crey find out about Cav?"

Cannon finishes his drink of coffee and lowers the white mug with *#1 Grandma* in a purple and pink swirly font to the table. "Dom Casso."

Dropping the crust of my toast on the edge of my plate, I wait for him to elaborate. He doesn't. "But that doesn't explain how you'd find out *now*. Did Dom go to Crey? Or did Crey go looking for information and seek out Dom?"

When Cannon doesn't answer right away, I know it's because he's weighing his answer against how much he really wants me to know. He never shows all his cards, but that's just Cannon.

"Crey tried to reach you shortly after you landed in Belize, but got no answer on your cell phone."

"I know. I didn't have service down there."

Cannon's eyebrow rises. "You didn't have service because Cav didn't want you to have service. We checked with the carrier. You should've automatically switched over to the local network. Since you've been sleeping for about eighteen hours, I've gone through all the settings on the phone with the provider, and it appears Cav switched the one you needed to hook up to the local network. He wanted you cut off from everyone, Greer."

My mind grapples with this revelation. First, how the hell did I sleep for eighteen hours? *Good God, woman.* And second, why would Cav do that?

The blows keep coming as Cannon continues. "The Internet was also disconnected in the house, and the caretakers were under orders from Cav not to relay any messages to you that Creighton was trying to reach you. He wanted you isolated from the rest of the world."

The piece of bacon I just picked up falls back to my plate. "Why?"

"How better to get into your head than cutting you off from your support system? It's a common technique to build rapport."

Common to kidnappers and cults, maybe. Could Cav really be so calculating? It only takes me a moment to answer my own question.

Yes. He is.

I can't forget I was a job from day one. Everything he's said and done has been calculating. And dammit, I gave him the exact opening he needed to come back into my life.

The anti-Cav train in my head derails around the next curveball question. *Why would he come back now?* I'm not a job anymore.

I decide to throw that one at Cannon's feet. "Why would he come back into my life and go to all this trouble? What's his end game? What does he want from me now?"

Cannon lifts *#1 Grandma* to his lips again and drinks before responding. "I don't know, but he has an angle. He always has an angle."

For a moment, I wonder if Cannon is talking about himself, because I truly believe that about him. But I have trouble, even in my raw state, attributing that to Cav. He doesn't seem cold and calculating. The opposite, actually. He seared me with the heat of his need, introduced me to pleasures I never knew existed.

But he lied. About everything. After you trusted him with the most vulnerable parts of you.

Betrayal is a cold blade slicing through the village of rationalizations I'm building in my head. I can't rationalize this away. The stabbing pain in the vicinity of my heart tells me that too.

"So, what now? I'm banished to the backwoods of Kentucky?"

Cannon rises from the table and rinses his mug in the sink. "You're laying low. If you want to call it banishment, that's your choice. But after that stunt on Twitter yesterday morning, you unleashed another media cycle tearing into your character, and stock prices are taking a hit. We need to distance you from the companies if you're going to keep acting like a spoiled little brat."

And there we have it, the unvarnished truth from the mouth of Cannon Grove himself.

As much as it frustrates me to have my actions scrutinized so heavily and affect Creighton's business, I know he's right.

"How do you distance me?"

"You transfer all your interest in the companies to someone else. If you're not a majority shareholder in so many of the businesses, then investors, after proper education, won't be so concerned by your actions."

Give up my interest in Karas Holdings? I remember the first time Creighton told me he was building the company, not only to secure his future, but to secure mine as well. He'd just taken a huge risk in the foreign currency market and made his first billion.

It wasn't the money that hit me hardest, it was the feeling of solidarity. Creighton and me against the world, just like it was always Creighton and me against my aunt and uncle. Even though I have limited knowledge of all the details, I've been a part of almost every business venture he's been involved in. When your brother is as busy and ambitious as mine, drawn in a hundred different directions at once, it's one way to know you still occupy an important spot in his life.

The purchase of Homegrown Records for Holly was one of the first business deals he excluded me from, but obviously I held no resentment. I understood completely.

But to me, giving up my interest in those companies is equivalent to giving up that bond with my brother. I don't want to do it.

I shake my head. "No. I'm not bowing out. I'll be better. No more drunken ad posting or tweeting. I'm done."

"Which is why you're here, and you've got no Internet and no cell phone. I grabbed the case file on your counter, so maybe that'll give you something else to do."

"So this really is exile? You want me cut off from everything." My words carry the weight of guilt I already feel. I'm twenty-six years old, and I'm still being treated like a child.

You did this to yourself, Greer. That inner voice is correct to a certain degree, but still . . . this is excessive.

"What about Banner? Can I at least talk to her?" I eye the old rotary telephone on the wall. It's definitely an antique, but I can figure out how to use it.

Cannon follows my line of sight. "Phone has been

shut off, and I've got a security guy coming in to babysit you while you're here. It might be best for you and Banner to take a little break from wreaking havoc on the world for a week or so."

"So I've been grounded. In Kentucky."

His smile is slightly less smug than I expect. "Consider it an extension of your vacation in a new and exotic location."

I open my mouth to deliver a witty and no doubt scathing retort, when a knock on the door interrupts us.

"And that's your new security detail."

"Why?"

Cannon heads to the door. "I have to get back to the city, so my availability for babysitting has come to an end."

After unlocking the ancient-looking dead bolt, he pulls the door open to reveal a man who blocks most of the light coming in from outside.

I lean to the side to try to get a better look. What I see is a stocky guy around five foot eight who's extending his hand to Cannon.

"Troy German reporting for duty, sir."

It's his choice of words and the emphasis on *sir* that give away his military roots. I'm sure of it. So sure I'd bet a nude photo for the press on it. Cringing as soon as the thought sweeps across my brain, I rise and head for the door to meet my new babysitter.

"Cannon Grove, and this is Greer Karas."

"The subject. Understood."

Awesome, I'm a subject now. Way to dehumanize the situation, Troy.

I give him a polite but forced nod and return to my Wonder Bread. As I crunch away, I listen halfheartedly as Cannon grills Troy again on things I'm certain he already has memorized. But knowing Cannon, if a single answer doesn't check out, this guy is *gone*. Cannon might be a controlling ass, but he's always looked out for me.

When he's satisfied, he invites Troy inside, but Troy declines.

"No, sir. I'll be stationed out front and periodically walking the perimeter to make sure the property is secure."

I assume Cannon finds nothing wrong with that because he nods, and the former military man turns and steps off the porch.

"Well, that was interesting."

Cannon shrugs. "He comes highly recommended, and I'm comfortable leaving him in charge of you. All joking aside, he's not your babysitter. He's here to protect you, discreetly."

"Protect me from what?"

Cannon's frown clues me in to the fact that I'm asking the wrong question. The correct question is *protect me from whom.*

"Cav," I whisper. "He's here to protect me from Cav."

A nod is all the confirmation I need. "He's here to make sure Mr. Casso doesn't decide to do anything stupid."

"His name is Westman."

"Only when it became convenient for him."

"You know more about him than I do, clearly. So, why

don't you share?"

A few beats pass before Cannon replies. "That's not my place. My job here is to make sure you've got someone you can count on to keep you safe. Now, is there anything else you need from me before I head back to the city?"

I open my mouth to deliver some snarky comment, but decide it's not worth it. Cannon thinks I'm a world-class fuckup, so why reinforce that opinion any more than I already have through my actions?

"No. Nothing." And because I still have the manners I was raised with, I add, "Thank you."

"Anytime, Greer. You know both your brother and I would do anything for you. Including saving you from yourself."

He could have left off that last little bit, *thank you very much*. I give him a pained smile and clear my breakfast dishes away. Cannon's already out the door and starting up his car when I realize there's no dishwasher. It's not until I'm finished cleaning up the kitchen that I discover I'm completely cut off.

Cannon was correct—the old rotary phone doesn't work. I have no cell. The cable is turned off. There's no Internet.

Every single one of those things was missing in Belize, and yet I didn't feel alone and deprived there because I had Cav.

And now I just have . . . me.

I can't read another page in this book. My second Danielle Steel isn't holding my attention. I've already read every detail of every page of Holly's yearbooks from high school—she was adorable, by the way—and now I'm going stir crazy. Is this what they mean when they talk about *cabin fever*? I have to get out of here.

I opened the front door three hours ago, only to be met by Troy German with a stern order to go back inside. When I tried to chat, he stonewalled me and pulled the door shut. I made myself lunch with the ample groceries Cannon left, but now I need to do something before I start tearing my hair out.

During lunch and between my Danielle Steels, I watched Troy's pattern around the house. Day is turning to dusk, and his pattern hasn't changed. He stays stationed out front for twenty minutes and then spends five minutes "walking the perimeter." Holly's gran's house doesn't sit on a vast piece of property. I have no frame of reference for how big it is, but it can't be much bigger than the footprint of my New York apartment building. Definitely not a city block.

So I start planning. Holly has told me the story about the night Creighton dragged her out of Brews and Balls, the bowling alley where she used to work and made her karaoke stage debut. I *think* Holly said it was less than a mile away.

I might be a city girl, but one thing I know I can do is walk. And if walking a mile gets me to some sort of civilization, then I'm down with it.

I dig through my available clothes, glancing out the

upstairs window as Troy makes another round in his perimeter walk. I slip into skinny jeans and a blouse, shove some cash and my ID in my pocket, and make my way down the stairs. Peering between the front blinds, I catch him climbing back into his SUV and shutting the door.

It's go time.

I'm breaking out.

Clearly, Troy doesn't expect me to make this kind of move, because when I slip out the back door and haul ass across the grass to the dirt road that runs behind the back of the lot, I don't hear him yelling. I duck behind a tree with a trunk double the width of my body and wait, my lungs heaving, for the shouts to come.

They don't.

I wait another twenty seconds, counting slowly in my head, before I peek around the tree. Still nothing. I make another break for it, sprinting on my ballet flats to pause behind a shed at the back of the next yard.

All I can hope now is that I'm going in the right direction.

CHAPTER
EIGHT

Greer

Twenty minutes later, I'm sure I'm lost. It's almost full dark and this country road isn't lit. I'm about to give up and turn back when I hear the thump of music in the distance and the glow of neon lights.

Thank you, universe.

I come around the side of the building to the front entrance and find Pints and Pins is written in large scrolling letters across the yellow block-and-sheet-metal building. *I thought Holly called it Brews and Balls?* But how many bowling alleys can there really be in Gold Haven, Kentucky?

Inside is a cacophony of sound as the crash of balls into pins, loud laughter, and blaring music engulf me. No one looks twice as I head toward the bar and grab a table— or so I think.

The harried waitress in her yellow-and-blue uniform takes my order—a cheeseburger, fries, and soda water with lime. I'm laying off the booze tonight, and probably forever if I were smart.

I'm congratulating myself on fitting in so well when a tall, broad-shouldered man in a red-and-black plaid flannel shirt takes a seat in the chair across from me without invitation. He lowers a frosty mug of beer to the chipped blue Formica table between us.

"She said I might see you here." His deep voice carries only a trace of an accent.

"Excuse me?"

"Holly."

I stare blankly at him, shock pooling in my belly while I consider how to respond. *He knows who I am. Do I lie? Pretend he's crazy?*

No, if he knows Holly, then chances are he could google my picture in a hot second and it would be very clear that I'm lying. I've had too many lies in my life lately to want to go down that route.

I embrace the truth instead as his brilliant blue eyes scan my appearance. "Did she tell you to call her when I staged a jailbreak?"

He laughs, and the deep, rich sound drowns out the rest of the noise in the bar. "Not exactly. She told me to keep an eye out for you and take you home if I found you walking the streets. She didn't expect you'd want to be babysat for too long."

The waitress brings my soda water and lime. After thanking her, I raise my glass in a toast to the man across the table from me.

"Cheers to not being babysat. I'm twenty-six years old and capable of looking after myself."

His chuckle has my gaze cutting to his blue eyes, which dance with humor when he says, "So I hear. You've done a bang-up job."

"Don't patronize me." My words are snappish, at best.

"And don't throw fancy words at me. I'm a simple country boy."

"Sure you are," I mumble.

"And apparently one with very bad manners." He reaches a hand across the table. "Logan Brantley, at your service, Ms. Karas."

I take his offered hand, and mine is surrounded by his much larger palm.

"Please call me Greer."

"Sure thing. Now, Greer, does your babysitter have any idea you're out enjoying Gold Haven's finest entertainment this evening?"

I swing my head toward the entrance out of instinct. Has Troy discovered my absence yet? I don't see the bull-like man storming through the doors, so I'm going to take that to mean my escape is still a successful secret.

I shake my head. "Nope."

"Well, damn, I guess you better enjoy it while you can."

"That's the plan. And find a phone so I can reach my best friend before she freaks out about where I am and loses her mind. She thought I'd be back in New York yesterday. And I would have been if Creighton hadn't wanted to keep me out of the way."

Logan produces an older model iPhone from his pocket. "It might not be the latest and greatest, but it'll get the job done." He slides it across the table toward me.

Glancing at him with surprise winding through me, I snatch up the phone and immediately open the messaging app. Banner's number is one of the few I have memorized, mostly because she had the number chosen specifically for her when we were fifteen. 212-669-6969. I tap in the number and work out a quick message.

> *It's G!! I'm alive!! I'm in Gold Haven, KY. They've got a security guy sitting on Holly's gran's house who thinks he's GI Joe. Basically, I'm being held hostage by boredom, so I sneaked out to have some real human interaction. This isn't my phone, but if you message me back in the next hour or so, I should still be with the guy.*

I send the text and stare at the screen, anxiously waiting for the gray bubbles that would signal she's texting back immediately. Nothing. *Come on, Banner. Where are you?*

I need my best friend's advice. I'm tempted to excuse myself to the ladies' room and call her, but Banner is quick on the trigger responding to text messages, unless she's busy with her latest conquest. Even then, I expect to hear from her soon.

Impatient, I lay the phone on the table between Logan and me, and look up to find his gaze on my face.

"Leave it there or go call her. Up to you. I'm the last

person to claim to be a babysitter." His easy nature drains a measure of my anxiety away.

The waitress returns with a tray holding two cheeseburgers, fries, and another beer for Logan. After she unloads it and walks away, Logan smiles.

"Hope you don't mind me joining you for dinner. Thought it might be better that way. Keeps the vultures from trying to land on the fresh meat."

Vultures?

I casually scan the room and find dozens of eyes on us. A solid fifty percent of them are on Logan, the eyes of all the females, but he's right, there are plenty of men looking at me like I'm as delicious as the burger in front of me appears to be.

Dropping my gaze back to my food, I shrug. "And here I thought I was flying below the radar."

Logan chugs a swallow of his beer before once again unleashing his deep chuckle. "I don't think you understand the true meaning of flying below the radar, sweetheart."

Picking up my burger with both hands, I lift it to my lips. "You might be right about that." I take a huge bite, holding back a moan at the deliciousness of it, then chew and swallow before adding, "I'm not sure you do either." I follow my words with a meaningful scan around the room at all the women who still have their eyes fixed on the attractive man across from me.

Logan digs into his own burger and washes the bite down with beer before he responds. "Most of the women in this town have one thing in common."

"What's that?"

"They didn't think I was good enough before I left for the military, and didn't think I was good enough when I came back from the military."

"So, what changed?" I sip my soda water and take another mammoth bite while I wait for his answer.

"Money," he says, his tone dripping with derision.

Honestly, the response doesn't surprise me a bit. "That happens. People come out of the woodwork when all of a sudden you've got what you didn't have before."

"They can all go straight to hell, for all I'm concerned. I'll take their money to work on their cars, but I'm not going to let myself get trapped by some chick who'll just try to get knocked up to get a child support payment out of me for eighteen years. Or even worse, the ones who think I'd marry them."

I've never before considered the intricacies of small town life. Never having lived it, I had no reason to. But now that Logan Brantley lays it out, it makes perfect sense. The women in this bar look at him like he's the golden ticket out of their paycheck-to-paycheck lives. Now that he's mentioned cars, I remember Holly talking about the garage he bought and expanded, and the cool work he did. She's way more of a car chick than I am, so I'm a little ashamed to admit most of that went in one ear and out the other.

But I think he's missing a major point. I set my hamburger down on the wax paper in the red plastic basket and pick up a french fry. "I think you're probably right to a certain extent, but to put it crassly, I also think there are a lot of women in here who probably just want to take you home and let you bang the hell out of them."

Logan chokes on his beer, and the mug lands on the table with a thump. He leans forward and coughs into his hand as I squeeze more ketchup into my basket for my fries and proceed to dip away.

"Did you learn your bluntness from Holly? Shit, woman."

I smile. "Actually, no. That comes from years of not being able to say what I think. I embrace the filterless lifestyle whenever I can get away with it. If you think I'm bad, you should meet my best friend, Banner."

"She's the one you texted?"

I nod, my gaze dropping to the phone between us that hasn't lit up with a response.

"She'll get back to you."

I smile weakly. "I hope so. But if she doesn't, at least she knows where I am so she won't freak out any more than necessary."

"And what about the press? You're supposed to be laying low."

"You shouldn't insult my friend by assuming she'd tell the press anything. She wouldn't. She's good people."

He holds up a hand in a placatory gesture. "Didn't mean any harm. I'm still recovering from your blunt-force honesty."

With a shrug, I grab another fry. "It's the truth. There are generally three camps of women—the ones who want what you've got to offer in bed—of which Banner is a perfect example, the ones who want what you've got in your bank account, and then the ones who just want you."

Logan's blue eyes fix on me. "Which camp do you belong in?"

"We're not talking about me."

I told myself when Cav walked into the picture that I could be in the first camp. Just have a fling and move on when it ended. And then in Belize, I started falling for the man the same way I did three years ago.

What is it about him? Why do I feel like being around him paints my life with a completely new layer of happy I can't get anywhere else?

"I don't even need you to answer to know you're one of the rare category-three women. And somehow I'm always a day late and a dollar short when it comes to finding them. You're really hung up on this Hollywood guy, aren't you?"

My head jerks up and a french fry goes flying across the table, narrowly missing Logan's arm to land on the floor.

"You don't have to throw food at me just because I'm right."

I bite my lip to stifle the laugh. "I can't believe I just did that." Standing, I move to clean it up, but Logan's hand stops me.

"Don't worry about it. It's not the first fry to end up on this floor, and it won't be the last."

He waits until I resettle in my seat to ask his question again. "So, it's serious with this guy? Holly seemed to think so."

"Does Crey know you talk to Holly about stuff like

this?" I have a hard time believing my possessive big brother would be cool with this guy being chatty with his wife.

"Who do you think told her to set up a second line of defense after you slipped away from the retired Rambo?"

Of course, Crey would.

"Look, I don't want to talk about Cav. I don't know what's going on there, mainly because . . . well, you can't build a relationship on a lie."

Logan pauses, his hand on his beer mug. "Normally I'd agree, but something drew you in about this guy. So, why would you give up that easily? Just throw in the towel and not demand an explanation?"

I shrug, my shoulders hunched over the plastic basket, my burger and fries suddenly looking less appetizing. "I'm not exactly in any position to demand an explanation while I'm on lockdown in Kentucky."

Logan lifts his beer to his lips, but before he drinks, he says, "I'm sure you'll get your chance, Greer. It's up to you what you make of it."

CHAPTER NINE

Cav

Banner was harder to find than I expected. I didn't have her number, and her office wouldn't give me her address—apparently New York isn't impressed with Hollywood fame, so I had to turn to social media. Thankfully, she posted a selfie a half hour ago and tagged the location.

I'm on the hunt, and I'm not leaving until I have a lock on Greer. Creighton Karas has the resources to send her anywhere, as is clear from our trip to Belize. But it's even more clear that Greer would *let* him send her anywhere. She follows her brother's orders too well, in my opinion, especially when his orders are contrary to mine.

This time, I won't give her a choice. She'll hear me out. I'm a man on a mission, and I'm willing to step over the line to get what I want from her. Greer has no idea what's coming, but she will soon.

I walk into Jamison's Pub, thankful that Banner isn't spending time at some ritzy martini bar where I'd be recognized within moments. Jamison's is a neighborhood bar, and it's packed tonight. She's sitting on the lap of a skinny guy who obviously has no idea what to do with a woman of her caliber. *Poor sap.* She'll take what she wants from him and won't leave her number in the morning. That's my expert assessment of the situation, anyway.

I stop at the end of the booth and clear my throat to get their attention. Banner pulls her mouth away from the man's neck, and he looks shell-shocked.

"Whoa, Hollywood. You got some hella big balls to stand in front of me. Hope you're ready to lose them." She hops off the man's lap and reaches for a dinner knife. "You fucked with the wrong girl, because I will cut you for hurting her."

A shard of guilt lances through me at the memory of Greer's face twisting in pain. It's the last thing I wanted, and yet I've always known it was inevitable. But she was supposed to let me pick up the pieces and fix things—not let her brother drag her off to God knows where.

"Uh . . . maybe you should put the knife down." This comes from the guy adjusting his glasses and trying to smooth his hair back into its faux-hawk style after being destroyed by Banner's wandering hands.

"No. This guy needs to pay."

She doesn't expect me to reach out and yank the knife away from her. Once I've liberated it, I slip it into my pocket.

"What the fuck, dude?"

"Where is she?"

Banner crosses her arms and glares at me mulishly. "Why would I tell you a damn thing?"

"Because I'm gonna make things right."

Uncrossing her arms, Banner props her hands on her hips and tilts her head. "How the hell could you possibly do that? From what I hear, you've been lying since day one. She trusted you with her ass, and you broke that sacred trust. There's no coming back from that."

The guy coughs out a laugh, and my gaze cuts to him. "You repeat a word of this conversation and you'll end up floating in the East River."

His eyes go wide, and a flash of appreciation lights up Banner's. Sensing my in, I seize it.

"I've done nothing but protect her. Even from myself. Let me fix this. Tell me where she is."

Banner's phone buzzes where it sits on the table.

"Is that her?" There's no ignoring my demand.

Banner picks up the phone. "I have no idea who it is."

"Check it."

She raises both eyebrows to her hairline. "You bossing me around is going to get you nowhere." Still, she unlocks her phone and checks the text message. She tries to keep her expression neutral, but I read more in it.

"It's her." My words aren't a question.

Banner nods. "Give me one good reason why I should tell you where she is."

I don't hesitate. "I love her."

She studies my face for several moments before holding out the phone. I reach for it, but she pulls it back before I can grab it. "If you fuck her over again, I will cut off your balls with a rusty knife. Is that clear?"

"Crystal."

Banner drops the phone in my hand, and I read the text before forwarding both it and the number to my own phone. Then I delete both texts without the slightest hint of remorse. Banner doesn't need to alert Greer to any of this.

I lock the phone and hand it back to her. "Thank you."

I'm pushing open the door of the bar when I hear Banner's screech of fury.

CHAPTER
TEN

Greer

I'm in Logan's truck at the four-way stop a couple hundred yards from Holly's gran's house.

"I wonder if he noticed I'm gone."

"He's a piss-poor security detail if he didn't." Logan's tone takes on a judgmental note.

I look across the cab of the truck at him. "You ever been security detail?"

He shrugs. "For some people who pissed off Uncle Sam, on occasion." He's mentioned his military service, so his answer isn't a surprise.

"Do you miss it?"

I ask the question to take my mind off the reentry I'm about to attempt. Nerves multiply in the pit of my stomach, and I'm doubly glad I stuck to my soda water and lime. Not only do I not need another hangover, I need to

58

have my wits about me when I confront Troy German.

Logan rolls through the four-way stop and keeps the speed of the truck down as we approach the little house with the black SUV out front.

"I miss the brotherhood. Feeling like I was part of something bigger than myself. But sweatin' my balls off in the desert and eatin' sand? No. Don't miss that."

As we slow in front of the house, I ask, "How are we going to do this?"

"Not much you can do but tell him the truth."

A grumble rises up from my throat. "Awesome. Great plan."

Gravel crunches beneath the tires as Logan pulls the truck into the yard next to the SUV. Troy throws his door open before we even come to a complete stop. Logan's windows are tinted, and with the help of the dark night, I hope I'm not visible yet.

Troy rounds the hood to knock on the driver's side window, and Logan rolls it down. "You need to—"

Whatever he's about to say dies when Logan turns on the interior lights and Troy sees me sitting in the passenger seat.

"*Fuck.*"

"She got bored. No one's going to tell the boss unless you do, so you might as well let me walk the lady up to the front door and let her get some rest," Logan drawls.

I, for one, think that sounds like an excellent idea, but who knows if straitlaced Troy is going to go for it. I hold my breath as I wait for his response.

"I've got relief coming in twenty minutes. She better

get inside. I'll tell him I just checked on her, so he won't need to disturb her."

My annoyance at being talked about like I'm not present is slightly mollified because he could be reaming me out, or worse—calling Creighton or Cannon, and then *they'd* ream me out. Somehow, in all of this, the men in my life have forgotten that I'm an adult, and I think tomorrow is the perfect time to remind them. I'm not spending another day cooped up in that house with no access to the outside world. I don't care what Creighton or Cannon say, I'm *done* with this nonsense. I'm ready to go back to New York and piece my life back together.

"Sounds like a plan, man," Logan says, reaching for the door handle. "I'll walk her up to the house, and no one will be the wiser."

"Who the hell are you anyway?" Suspicion enters Troy's tone.

"Friend of the family. Mrs. Karas told me to keep an eye on her."

Troy studies him closely as though he's a human lie detector. Finally appeased, he steps back so Logan can open the door. Logan comes around to the passenger side and opens mine as well.

He holds up a set of keys as we make our way up the front walk. "I'm assuming you didn't bring any with you."

My gaze darts to the front door, and I realize just how poorly I planned this little outing. "Um. Yeah, nope. Thank you."

Logan nods, explaining, "Holly has me come check on the place at least once a week."

"You're a nice guy, Logan Brantley." I stop on the purple front porch and turn to face him. "Thank you for everything."

His grin is quick and easy. "I ain't that nice. Take care of yourself, Greer. Holler if you need anything. My number is on the pad by the phone inside." After he unlocks the door, he gives me a quick hug and pushes me inside.

I'm alone with my thoughts as I get ready for bed. I won't admit that I'm missing Cav something fierce tonight.

He lied to me.

Attempting to harden my heart while it's cracked into pieces is a lot like trying to wash a broken window. Pointless. There's not a damn thing I can do about it now, though. My time is better spent wondering why the hell Banner didn't answer my text. *I really hope it's not another carny . . .*

I tidy up my little room, packing most of my stuff. Regardless of the law Creighton laid down, I'm done being stashed away like I'm an embarrassment. I'm going home tomorrow, come hell or high water.

When I slip into bed, I miss the heat of Cav's body beside me. *Stupid heart. Stupid body. Ugh. Stupid girl.*

I fall asleep telling myself I'm going to get over him tomorrow.

CHAPTER
ELEVEN

Cav

Six hours after I leave Banner at the bar, I'm standing in the shadows of a small white farmhouse in Bumfuck, Kentucky, with a duffel bag over my shoulder and my rental SUV idling quietly on the dirt road behind the property.

I've been watching the place for over an hour, and this security guy deserves to be fired. He never varies his routine at all. As soon as he's back in the sedan, I start my mental timer.

I pull the lock-pick set from my back pocket and dredge up my old skills as I climb the steps to the back door. A few manipulations of the lock, and the handle turns freely.

Silence greets me as I step inside the house. I pause in the dark kitchen to listen but hear nothing. My eyes adjust to the darkness as I move from room to room on the main floor. Empty.

Adjusting the bag on my shoulder, I find the back stairs that lead to the second floor and take them two at a time, hoping to miss old and creaky steps. I'm mostly successful. I pause again at the top of the stairs, but still hear nothing. There are only two doors in the short hallway and I choose the one to my right, pushing it open soundlessly.

The shape in the bed tells me everything I need to know. Greer sleeps curled up like that when she doesn't have me wrapped around her.

Still silent, I move to the side of the bed and lay out the contents of the bag on the floor—everything I need to keep her quiet and get her out of the house undetected.

She'll forgive me. Eventually.

I buckle restraints around her ankles and wrists before Greer comes fully awake. She doesn't have a chance to scream before I push the gag into her mouth and secure it.

This isn't your normal breaking and entering. No, this is a kidnapping.

CHAPTER
TWELVE

Greer

I wake to the feel of something being shoved in my mouth and latched around the back of my head. I reach for my face, but my hands are bound. My ankles too.

What the fuck?

Alarm bells are clanging in my head when my eyes blink open in time to see a masked man, all in black, just before he ties a blindfold around my eyes. He knots the silky fabric tight behind my head and I scream, but the rubber ball in my mouth stifles the sound.

Oh. My. Fucking. God.

I struggle, kicking out with my bound feet. *Useless.*

My muffled screams come in earnest when I'm lifted off the bed and lowered onto some sort of cushion, my arms and legs folded into place. Canvas fabric surrounds me as the sound of a zipper penetrates the ringing in my brain.

Oh my God, I'm being zipped into a bag.

My entire body is jostled when the bag rises from the floor. A low grunt is the only noise in the room as the man starts from the room.

That's when the reality of the situation hits me. *Holy. Fuck. I'm being kidnapped.*

Having a billionaire for a brother and more money than most people could imagine in my own right, I know I'm a target for kidnapping. My best defense against this, in my opinion, has always been the anonymity presented by living in the city. I can go mostly anywhere and not be recognized.

But here in Gold Haven, I don't have that luxury.

My mind spins in a hundred different directions. *Is it some redneck from the bar? A few of them looked like they wanted to make me their backwoods bride. Someone who wants a ransom? An enemy of Creighton's? Who?*

And where the hell is my security?

I bounce against the hard body of the man as we make our way down what I assume has to be the stairs.

Shit, if he gets me out that door, I'm screwed.

All the horrific possibilities rip through my brain. *White slavery. Rape. Torture. Ransom.*

The back door creaks open, and I kick my bound legs against the canvas fabric, wriggling for everything I'm worth. A heavy smack lands on the outside of the bag in the vicinity of my hip.

The asshole just hit me. He's going to die.

Between the temperature change and the squeaking

hinges, I know I'm outside. My chances of getting out of this unscathed are dropping with every fraction of a second.

The acrid scent of exhaust hits my nostrils moments later as I hear an idling engine and the sound of a door opening. I'm lifted higher before the bag is lowered onto another padded surface. I struggle, but can't find anything to grab with my bound hands.

The doors slam shut, and I know I'm fucked.

My name is Greer Karas, and I've just been kidnapped.

The drive is short, but the panic building in every cell of my body multiplies exponentially with each mile. Taking deep breaths, I try to push down the hysteria that's bubbling up. I need to find my cool, capable self, because I know fear isn't going to help.

But fuck that rational stuff—I'm in some kind of bag in the back of a van or an SUV. I run my hands along the inside of the zipper, my nails picking at the teeth, trying to tear it open. No luck. The car slows and speeds up. Turns left and right. I'm completely lost.

Shit. Even if I can get out of this bag and kick out the taillights like that *Dateline* episode suggested, how am I going to ever find my way back?

Repositioning my body, I use my feet to push at the zipper, hoping to rip it open. I have to get out. Nothing budges. My scream of frustration is muted almost to nothing by the gag. No sound comes from the driver of the vehicle.

Or maybe he's the passenger? Whoever he is, he's going to die a slow and painful death when my brother gets his hands on him.

The vehicle finally slows to a halt. Other noises come from outside, and I hope like hell it's people who can help me. I'm in Gold Haven, Kentucky, for God's sake, not Rio or Tijuana. *This can't happen here!*

Fear grips my muscles with paralyzing claws as the rear door opens and a whoosh of colder air fills the back of the vehicle. No words are spoken when my bag is tugged closer to the door and hefted once again.

Shit. Shit. Shit.

I scream against my gag, clawing and kicking at the inside of the bag. The sound of airplanes sends bolts of terror spiraling through me.

Holy. Fuck.

No one is ever going to see or hear from me again. I'm going to be sold to some fat sheik like in the movie *Taken*. My brother is amazing, but he's no Liam Neeson. Maybe he knows Liam? Hysteria is jumbling my thoughts, and my fear edges into full-on breakdown territory.

I'm going to die. I'm never going to see my family again. I'm never going to see Banner. I'm never going to know my baby niece. I'm never going to see Cav again and demand an explanation.

And that's when I hear the voice. *His* voice. I freeze.

"We ready for takeoff?"

"In just a few minutes. You need help with the bag, Mr. Westman?"

"No, I've got it."

Cav.

Relief sweeps through me, followed immediately by rage.

I'm going to kill him.

Kill. Him. Dead.

All the adrenaline that's been tearing through my veins over the last who-knows-how-many minutes morphs into the most vicious anger I've ever felt.

I'm. Going. To. Kill. Him.

With my bare hands.

My tirade is muted by the gag, but my struggles become violent.

He lands a slap on the bottom of the bag, this time on my ass. "Stop."

I still, but only because I'm saving my energy to go nuclear on him as soon as he unzips this thing.

How could he do this? I've never felt such gut-wrenching fear. Why is it that every encounter with Cav Westman, or Casso, or whoever the hell he is, drags more emotion out of me than any other encounter over the course of my life? It's insane.

He's insane.

And I'm insane for falling for him so blindly.

The word *falling* grabs me by the throat. I'm *not* falling. I'm getting over him.

Or I'm going to just kill him.

CHAPTER
THIRTEEN

Cav

I lower the duffel bag to the plane's carpeted floor and reach for the zipper. This is a little like taking the lid off a snake charmer basket.

Greer is going to come out looking for blood. It's the Karas in her. And I can't say I'm not looking forward to the battle that's about to come.

She doesn't fear me. She's strong and beautiful and as frustrating as hell, and I wouldn't change a damn thing about her. But that doesn't mean I won't use any means at my disposal to win back her trust. And I'm not letting her go until I have it.

It may seem counterintuitive to kidnap someone to get them to trust you again, but desperate times call for desperate measures. And when it comes to Greer, I'm willing to do whatever it takes. She's the ultimate prize, and

I'm not above fighting dirty to get what I want.

I kneel and reach for the zipper. Who am I kidding? I'm already fighting dirtier than my girl has ever seen. For a moment, the only sound in the cabin of the jet is the *hiss* of the zipper. I peel open the sides of the bag and the first thing I see is Greer's big, dark eyes blinking against the sudden brightness. Apparently my blindfold-tying skills need some work.

Once she stops blinking, her face screws into a determined expression as I lean down.

Wrong move. She jerks forward, attempting to head butt me. I dodge her move and wrap my palm around the back of her head, gripping her long dark hair in my fist.

"Whoa, baby girl. You've got some serious anger issues that we need to work out."

We've all heard the saying *if looks could kill . . .* I'm sure of one thing where Greer is concerned—she wants to do me some kind of bodily harm right now. A flash of guilt stabs into me for scaring her so badly, but I push it away. If she hadn't walked out of the house in Belize with her brother, none of this would be necessary.

I reach for the buckle on the gag. "Are you going to be a good girl so I can take this off?"

Her body relaxes several degrees, and her gaze loses its murderous intent.

"I'm taking that as a yes." After I unbuckle the gag, I pull it away from her mouth. The murderous glare is back.

"You motherfuck—"

I shut her up the best way I know how. After the gag, that is.

Crushing my lips to Greer's, I take what I want from her. It feels like coming home. *Fuck, I've missed this. Missed her. So goddamned much.* The tension that's been dogging me loosens now that I'm tasting her again.

Her sharp teeth nip my lip, *hard*, and I draw back.

"You kidnapped me! You're *insane*."

"Only because your brother keeps security on you, and I had to get you out undetected. I wasn't trying to scare the hell out of you. What else was I supposed to do? Ask your brother's permission? That's not how I work."

I lift her from her seated position, arms and legs still bound, and carry her to the bench seat on the left side of the cabin. Settling into the plush leather, I turn her sideways on my lap. We have a few minutes before takeoff, and I'll need to strap her into her seat without the captain noticing the restraints. Then again, he's paid well not to ask questions.

Squeezing tighter, I pull her into my body, crushing her against me. "Goddammit, I missed you, baby girl. How the hell could I fix this if I couldn't even get to you? You walked out, and I had no other option."

The last thing I expect to see is tears in her eyes, but they appear, turning her dark gaze glassy.

"But you did scare the hell out of me! I thought I was being stolen and sold to some fat sheik."

I smooth her wild hair out of her face. "Fuck, baby. I'm so goddamn sorry. I'd take that back if I could. If anyone ever tried to take you from me, I'd lie, cheat, and kill to get you back."

Greer buries her face in my neck, and I expect an

emotional scene. Instead, I feel teeth against my shoulder just before she bites down.

Wrapping my fist around her hair once again, I tug her head back.

"Listen to me. I swear on my life, I would never let anything happen to you. Three years ago, you knew I wasn't like any guy you'd ever met before. I'm still not like them. As far as I'm concerned, you belong to me, Greer, and there's no way in hell I'm letting your brother stash you somewhere I can't get in contact with you. There's only one person I trust with your safety—me. I will always protect you."

She unleashes a sound somewhere between a howl and a scream of frustration as she struggles against me.

Fuck it. I'm following my gut.

CHAPTER
FOURTEEN

Greer

One moment I'm thrashing against Cav, determined for him to feel something approaching what I went through in that damn bag, and the next moment I'm face-down on his lap with my sleep shorts tugged down.

I don't have time to react before his palm lands on my ass with a *slap*. I suck in a breath to scream, but it doesn't make it to my lips.

He lands smack after smack on my ass, and I forget about everything else except for the spot every strike lands. I focus on the pain, the burn, the need for more.

How is it possible this is calming me down and centering me rather than sending me into another blind rage?

I shift against Cav's lap again, but this time, it's because of the growing heat between my thighs.

There's something wrong with me. I shouldn't react like

this.

But there's no getting around it because I am. I love how he takes me in hand and doesn't ask permission. Cav is giving me something I didn't know I needed until that exact moment.

By the last few strikes, I'm arching into his touch. Seeking it. Needing it. How is it possible for me to forget all of his transgressions the moment he puts his hands on me?

Whether I'll admit it to him or not, I can at least admit it to myself—I missed him. All of him. Why do I crave his kinks? Is this why I've never been satisfied with a sexual relationship before? Because I needed this . . . dirty little extra? Or is it because I just needed Cav?

I arch up, expecting another blow, but instead his palm lands softly on my ass and kneads my skin. The burn intensifies with every squeeze. When his fingers slip between my thighs, I know exactly what he's going to find, and I nudge them open wider.

Shameless in this moment, I want him to feel how wet he makes me. I want my man to know how badly I need him right now, how badly I want him to fill me up with his fingers, and then his cock, and help me block out these last days of confusion and frustration.

I want to forget the bombs of truth Creighton dropped on us and go back to being the us that we were in Belize before that morning. I want all the things I told him I wanted—the things I thought I could actually have for those few days.

Can that ever be my reality? Or is this doomed to be

nothing but a fantasy?

When Cav slides a finger through my slickness, I know this is no fantasy. This is real, and I need him. *Now*.

I open my mouth to beg, but Cav pulls my shorts up, flips me over, and settles me on the seat beside him.

The cockpit door, already half-open, swings open the rest of the way.

"We're ready for takeoff, Mr. Westman. Please make sure your seat belt is fastened."

The pilot doesn't make eye contact with either of us, and I'm grateful. A flush spreads along my cheekbones as I think of what he might have witnessed had Cav not been so quick to move me.

When Cav buckles me in and the plane begins to move forward, my hands are still bound behind my back. "I'll get you loose after we take off, as long as you think you can behave."

His lifted eyebrow doesn't make me want to slap the expression off his face anymore. There's something else I want from him right now.

"I don't care if you keep me bound as long as you make it worth my while."

A flash of surprise streaks across his face, but it doesn't last long before his greenish-gray eyes heat.

"You want me to take care of that wet little pussy? Make you come? On my fingers, my face, and then with my cock?"

I shift on my seat, pressing my thighs together to ease the ache he's caused.

"Ah, baby girl. We've got a long flight, so you better

believe I'm going to take you every way I want to."

"Where—"

Cav presses a finger to my mouth to silence me. "No questions." He trails the pad of his index finger along my lower lip. "Now, suck."

He's a brave man when only minutes ago I was trying to bite him. But he's gambled correctly because right now I don't want to bite that finger. I'll use it to make his need rival mine. He's going to lose his mind with hunger for me. Besides, I want that finger intact so he can fuck me with it and make me come.

Greedy? Who cares. I'm the one who got kidnapped and spent some of the longest minutes of my life in gut-wrenching fear. I deserve several orgasms to make up for it. Our come-to-Jesus talk can wait. Right now, I just want Cav. I might still want to kill him later, but not right this moment.

I suck his finger into my mouth, laving it with my tongue and lips and dragging lightly down it with my teeth.

As we hurtle down the runway, I make promises to him with my eyes. *Take the restraints off or don't; I'm still going to want you.*

Cav reaches out with his other hand and cups my breast, covered only by the soft material of my thin T-shirt. Chill bumps prickle along my skin when his fingers close around my nipple and twist.

A moan escapes my lips, and I press into his touch. We say nothing until the captain announces that we've reached our cruising altitude.

Cav removes his seat belt and mine before hauling me back onto his lap.

"Jesus Christ, woman. Feel what you did to me."

He presses his hips up and against me, and I wiggle my ass against his cock's solid length.

"I want it."

"Good, because I'm going to lower you onto your knees, unzip my pants, and help you take it down your throat. And then I'm going to lift you up on my lap and slide your pussy down my cock until you're full of me."

His dirty talk kills me every time.

"What are you waiting for?" I ask, my tone taking on a seductive depth.

"Need to taste you again first."

His lips crush to mine, and his tongue dives inside without waiting for invitation. Cav kisses like he does everything else—throwing his whole self into it. His hand is buried in my hair, tilting my head the way he likes. I moan into his mouth, loving the urgency radiating from him.

Finally, he pulls my head back, his eyes greener than before. "On your knees, baby girl."

I nod as he helps me to the floor, the plush carpeting cushioning my position. Cav unzips his jeans and fists his cock as he pulls it out. As I lean forward, my hair falls around my face, but with my bound hands, I'm helpless to pull it back.

Cav wraps one hand around the tangled strands and clenches it behind my head. I'm at his mercy, and yet I've never felt more powerful. The need in his eyes burns into me, and I want to give as much as I want to take.

CHAPTER

FIFTEEN

Cav

She's fucking beautiful. A goddess, and yet she's kneeling at my feet. I don't deserve this woman, but I won't hesitate to take every advantage to ensure I can keep her in my life.

Greer's lips close over my cock, and my hands in her hair help guide her movements. *Fuck*. The nights that I was away from her, refusing to believe I'd never get her back, I dreamed of all the things we did in that house in Belize.

She sucks my cock with enthusiasm, as if working me over and making me come before I'm ready is going to gain her a prize. I can't complain, though. I'll let her try and when I'm about ready to blow, I'll tug her perfect mouth back and follow through on the rest of my promise.

Just the thought of sinking into her pussy has my balls

drawing up around the base of my dick. This is going to be a hell of a lot shorter ride than I planned.

I give her another minute before I pull her up into a standing position and tug her flimsy little shorts down her legs. They're still bound at the ankles, which puts a wrench in my plans.

Unless . . . I turn her around and pull her ass onto my lap, her pussy centered over my cock.

"You want this?" I shift so the head is tucked between her legs, nudging at her entrance.

"Yes," she whispers as she sinks down and takes it all. "*Fuuck . . .*"

"Oh my God."

Our words are lost as I grip her hips to lift and lower her over my cock, helping her ride me and take me deeper with every thrust.

Greer's head drops back, her hair spilling down around her shoulders.

I reach further around her hip and press two fingers down on her clit, wanting her orgasm to come fast and hard before I lose my own control. She grinds herself against my fingers with every stroke, her moans growing louder and louder. She's on the edge, and her pussy is clamping down on my cock.

"You're coming with me," I order.

"Yes," she says on a moan. "Now."

I fuck my hips upward harder into her and pull her down at the same time, unleashing both our climaxes.

Greer's head falls forward, and our hearts hammer in time for long, unmoving moments.

"You okay, baby?"

She nods, dropping her head backward onto my shoulder.

"We need to get you cleaned up."

She nods again, and I wish I'd had the forethought to grab something to clean up with. Spying cocktail napkins on the table next to the couch, I lean us both over and snag them before handing them to Greer. I help her stand and clean up before unbuckling the restraints on her ankles and arms, and knead her muscles and joints.

"Bathroom is in the back. Your other bag is under the seat. I grabbed it from the bedroom so you'd have clothes."

Apparently that was the wrong thing to say. Greer's head snaps around and her gaze lands on me, fury and hurt dominating once again.

"I still can't believe you freaking *kidnapped me*."

"I did what I had to do. I needed you out of there, and I wasn't going to ask your brother's babysitter for permission."

She shakes her head. "You could've knocked on the door like a normal person, and after I'd cried a little, I might have let you in. But no, you had to be the badass mobster's kid and break into the house, tie me up, *gag me*, and stuff me into a fucking bag. Who does that?" Hysteria invades her tone, and I infuse mine with authority.

"Go clean up. We'll talk about this when you're done."

Greer's expression hardens into a cool mask. "I don't know why you think I'm taking orders from you. You don't own me. You might have said that you love me, but I've never felt rage like I did the moment after I realized I wasn't being sold into white slavery and instead was being terrorized by someone I thought I could trust once upon a time. You lied to me, and I can see it in your face—you've got no remorse."

"You're right. I lied. I don't regret it. I wouldn't change a thing because it meant I got to have this time with you. You can expect me to play by your rules all you want, Greer, but it's never gonna happen."

Her hands ball into fists, and she drops her gaze to the carpet. When she looks me in the eye again, it's with a straight spine and the posture of a queen.

"And the phone and Wi-Fi? Cannon said you messed with it to keep me cut off. Like some kind of crazy person."

She may expect me to lie again, but I won't. "I had to keep the outside world away. We needed that time to figure out what could be possible for us."

Greer studies my face, dissecting my answer. "And you'd do it again, wouldn't you?"

"I'll do whatever it takes. When you're the prize, there's no lines I won't cross."

Her eyes narrow. "I'm no one's prize. Go fuck yourself, Cav."

I'm not expecting the slap, so when it lands on my cheek, my head snaps sideways.

She walks with dignity toward the bathroom at the back of the plane, and I wonder if I'm going to be able to dig my way out of this.

Her words echo in my head. *I've never felt rage like I did . . .*

Moments later, the sound of quiet sobs escape from

the bathroom, gutting me. *Fuck.*

After making quick work of the lock on the door, I pull it open and Greer is hunched over the vanity, her shoulders shaking as she cries out all the emotions of the last few days. I pull her into my arms but she struggles, beating against my chest.

"I hate you. I hate how you make me feel. Why do you do this to me? It wasn't enough to crush me three years ago? You had to come back and do it again? What kind of sick bastard are you?"

Her fists connect with my chest over and over, and her tears soak my T-shirt. But I say nothing and hold her tighter.

I'm not letting her go.

CHAPTER
SIXTEEN

Greer

I'm not this girl, the one who breaks down and cries in bathrooms. I'm not prone to outrageous emotional displays, crying jags, or pounding against a man's chest as I tell him I hate him. But somehow, I've become this girl with Cav.

Is it because I've never felt anything so strongly before him? That means something. Doesn't it? Have I been floating through life on this boring plateau where my emotions were always on the level, barely veering up or down? Do I want to go back to that? The colorless world where everything is fine and acceptable rather than amazing, but sometimes gut-wrenching?

You can't have the sweet without the bitter, and as much as I want to tell Cav to stop screwing with my heart and my head, I already know what my life is like without him.

Gray. Bleak. *Acceptable.*

I want more than that. And dammit, I want him, even if he's crazy enough to think kidnapping me is a good plan.

With that realization, my pounding fists become grasping fingers that curl into his shirt and draw him closer. His arms tighten around me, one hand cupping the back of my head and pulling it to his shoulder.

Can I accept this? Him? Even with the lies he has told me?

I know myself well enough to realize I can't move forward with him until I let go of the anger and betrayal.

Tears continue to fall, but instead of tears of anger, there's a cathartic force behind them. When they subside, Cav's grip on my hair loosens and I lift my head to meet his gaze.

"What are we doing?" I whisper the question in an unsteady tone.

"Working on having something beautiful."

"Do you think that's even possible for us?"

"You have to fight through the darkness to appreciate the beauty in the light. That's what we're doing. Fighting through the dark shit between us so we don't take for granted what's on the other side. If it were easy, would it be as special?"

His words make a weird sort of sense, and even though they don't seem like typical Cav, his serious expression says he means them absolutely.

"How do we get there?"

Smoothing his hand through my hair again, he tilts

my head back further. "We start over. A new beginning where we leave the past behind."

The concept is as seductive as it is simple.

"The past has its claws hooked deep in us."

Cav releases me before setting me away from him a step. "Are you more than Creighton Karas's little sister?"

I blink at the sudden change in subject and tone. "Maybe not to everyone, but absolutely."

"There are a hell of a lot of reasons I left New York, but the most compelling one is the fact that I'm not just Dom Casso's bastard kid. That's my past. It has nothing to do with who I am now. I don't take orders from him. I don't fall in line. My future is a lot bigger than the life I had in New York. In Hollywood, I'm Cav Westman. I'm my own man, and I've worked my ass off to become the kind of man you could respect. I've made my way on my own merit, not with my name, my connections, or anything else."

I understand what he's saying and can respect it, because as long as I stay in New York, I'll always be Creighton Karas's little sister. Be catered to because of my name and my connections. Any job I get will be obtained through the network my family ties allow me to be part of. The idea of stepping outside that bubble into a world where I have to make my way solely on my own merit like Cav did is equal parts terrifying and invigorating.

Can I do it? Am I going to have that chance? Cav is watching me, waiting for a response.

My reply is completely honest. "You've always been the kind of man I could respect, Cav. You didn't have to change anything for that."

His gaze drops to the floor for a beat before meeting mine again. "You know what I mean."

"I think you've always been harder on yourself than anyone else would ever be."

He shrugs and turns the conversation back to his point. "So, what do you say, Greer? Fresh start? New beginning? You and me trying to make something real together? No pretending this time."

He holds out his hand, offering it to me. All I have to do is take it, and he'll lead me out of the darkness and into the light.

It's time.

As I reach out and wrap my fingers around his, the anger I've been harboring since the morning I left Belize releases.

No pretending this time.

CHAPTER
SEVENTEEN

Greer

It's not quite daylight when we step down the stairs of the plane onto the tarmac. A black SUV waits for us twenty feet away, a driver in a suit standing next to the open door.

Cav and I were both quiet after my epic breakdown on the plane. So many thoughts battered my brain as I changed into clothes more suitable than my pajamas. Yes, I've agreed to a new beginning and let go of my anger, but the rawness of my feelings hasn't disappeared quite yet. Trust is a fragile thing, and gluing the pieces together of something that has already broken twice before is a difficult task.

I want to trust Cav, I really do, but it's going to take time. No pretending, which means I need to get there for real. He can say all the right things, but I need to see them in action before my instinctive wariness will fade.

Cav helps me into the SUV and hands my duffel bag to the driver to stow in the back before sliding into the black leather captain's chair beside mine. The driver climbs into his seat and shuts the front door. He rattles off an address, and Cav confirms it's correct.

I've been to LA before, but never to Hollywood, so this is going to be a completely new experience for me. New beginning. New life.

Can it really be so easy?

As the driver navigates out of the private airport, Cav reaches over and grabs one of the hands folded in my lap. Linking his fingers with mine, he brings it between us and squeezes.

"This isn't the first time I've imagined what it would be like to bring you home."

Home. Cav's home. I'm curious as hell about what his place will tell me about the man. He's been in my space—hell, he watched me from afar, studying me and learning my habits before I even knew he existed. I'm so far behind when it comes to Cav. Maybe this is my chance to find out everything he's hidden from me—and what I couldn't learn in the media.

The SUV curves around turns up into the hills until the driver pulls into a driveway blocked by a gate. Every house on this street has a gate, so apparently that's nothing out of the ordinary. The driver must be well versed in gate etiquette because he pulls up far enough so Cav can slide down the passenger window and type in the code on the keypad. The gate swings open, and the driver pulls in and parks before hopping out and opening my door.

He offers me a hand. "Miss?"

I accept it and climb out, memorizing every detail of the exterior of the house while I wait for Cav.

Like many other houses we passed on the way in, it's Spanish-style architecture with cream-colored stucco walls and a terracotta curved-tile roof. More terracotta tiles cover the arched overhang of the front entryway. No garage doors face the street, so I have to assume they're off to the side where the driveway swings around. Small shrubs and ornamental trees dominate the landscaping. It's not fancy, and I assume it's drought resistant. The lawn is green, but not as lush and vibrant as my aunt and uncle's estate.

After he thanks the driver and tosses the strap of my bag over his shoulder, Cav snags my hand and leads me toward the door. He releases me to dig into his pocket for a set of keys and after he unlocks the door, he pushes it open and I get my first look at Cav's home.

It's quiet. No voices come from inside, so I assume we're alone. There's furniture, but not much. It barely looks lived in. The grand idea that I'd glean many details from Cav's living space dies a quick death.

"Do you spend much time here?" I ask the question as I crane my head around doorways and see nothing that screams *Cav lives here* to me.

"Mostly only when I'm between projects or shooting on a studio set. I bought it fully furnished, basically move-in ready."

The Spanish-influenced furniture doesn't say Cav to me either, so I assume I'm going to learn more about Cav from him rather than from a house he bought fully furnished and apparently changed very little.

The man is still a mystery. I want his whole story, and not only because he has mine. In order to trust him, I need to understand him.

My tour is cut short as he leads me down a long hallway into a bedroom that I assume is the master. The large four-poster bed reminds me of Belize. *How many women has he tied to it before?* Cav is no choirboy, so I'd be an idiot to assume I'm the first. *But I can be the last.*

The thought materializes in my brain from out of nowhere. *Is that where we're headed? Forever territory?* I swallow back my shock because, honestly, when I think about my future, I picture Cav as part of it.

He drops my bag on the bench at the foot of the bed. "Tired?"

Taking stock of my body and my brain, I consider his question. I'm exhausted—physically, mentally, and emotionally—after the night I had. From the bowling alley to being kidnapped and a cross-country flight.

"A little."

"Why don't you try to sleep for a couple hours? I need to call my director and get the schedule for the scene we need to fix a voice-over on, and then I'll give you the rest of the grand tour and we can order in some food."

My eyes snap to his. "Voice-over?"

"Yeah. According to the director, the nearest mic failed, and we need to record voice-overs for the lines in the last scene. That's what I needed to get back for. We're recording it tomorrow."

All this Hollywood stuff is fascinating to me. I've never had any clue how movies are made.

"So you're going to go hang with famous people? Other famous people." I quickly correct myself because even though Cav has become regular-guy Cav to me, he's still a big freaking deal to most of the world. Especially the female half.

"Not quite yet. I just need to find out what the timing is so I make sure I'm there. They wanted to do it a couple days ago, but I had to put them off."

"Because you'd already planned a kidnapping?" My tone is dry rather than accusing.

Cav fights his grin but fails. "Something like that. Told them I had plans I couldn't reschedule."

I'm not sure I could roll my eyes any harder. "I bet." A yawn escapes me, and I glance at the bed.

"Go on, baby. I'll be here when you wake up. With food. How's that sound?"

Sleep and then food? Yes. Please.

"Perfect."

He leans in and presses a kiss to my forehead. "Get some sleep."

After Cav pulls the bedroom door shut, I strip and slide between the silky-soft sheets and the light-as-a-cloud blanket.

I'm in Cav's bed. In Cav's house. In Cav's town. It's surreal.

But that doesn't stop me from falling asleep within minutes.

CHAPTER EIGHTEEN

Greer

When I finally wake, I hear voices. The dark curtains blocking the sunlight give me no indication of how long I've slept. I look to the nightstand for a clock and find nothing.

Sitting up in bed, I yawn and stretch before sliding my legs over the side. My clothing choices are limited, so I grab a pair of leggings out of the duffel as well as a chambray shirt.

Once I'm dressed, I pull open the bedroom door and step barefoot into the hallway. I hear voices from inside the house, and it sounds like they're coming from a room on the opposite side as the bedroom. The closer I get, the more I'm convinced it's a TV playing and not actual people.

Peeking my head inside a study of some sort, I'm

proven wrong.

Cav sits with his feet propped up on the desk, leaning back in a chair, and a gorgeous blonde stands in the corner, one hand on her hip, gesturing with the other as she carries on a tirade.

Whoa. What the hell?

Cav spots me first, and his feet leave the desk and hit the floor. He sits up straight, and the blonde's head jerks around to the doorway.

Windsor Reed. I've seen her before. When I googled Cav's name and all the elegant red carpet pictures would show up, she was most often on his arm. I hated her with a burning fury that only irrational hate can have.

"Well, I guess this means it really is over, lover." She drawls the words, clearly meant for Cav, but they're directed at me.

"Stop it, Win. You're going to give her the wrong idea, and trust me, I don't need that shit from you."

She throws her blond mane back and laughs. It's like watching a Pantene commercial in real life—because she *does* the Pantene commercial. Stunning blue eyes go along with the thick blond hair and bombshell figure. If there was anyone born to be famous, it is this woman. Actually, I'm pretty sure her mother and father are both famous as well.

"You already in the doghouse with this one?" She continues to study me as she talks to Cav.

"None of your damn business." Cav shoves out of the chair and crosses the room to draw me against his side.

"Probably because she's out of your league."

I choke out a laugh at her ridiculous statement. "Excuse me?"

She ignores my bullfrog-like croak and holds out a hand as she steps toward me. "Windsor Reed. It's a pleasure to meet you . . ."

She lets her words trail off, fishing for a name. The polite side of me automatically fills it in and shakes her hand.

"Greer Karas."

Our handshake freezes mid-pump. "You're the billionaire's sister."

I cringe at the description. Like Cav said—I'm more than that. I'm an actual human being in my own right.

"My brother is rather infamous," I say instead.

"No, screw the brother. You're the one who got away, and this poor bastard moped for . . ." She looks to Cav. "How long did you mope? And then you got all determined."

Cav's look is hard and pointed. "That's enough."

"What? You don't want her to know you were worthless and pathetic for months and months because you had to leave her in New York?" She raises two fingers and presses them between her eyebrows. "This is the kind of stuff that's helpful to mention when you're trying to win a woman over, Westie. Get with the program."

She shakes her head, drops her hand, and looks at me in female commiseration. "Men aren't always the brightest creatures, and then put some tits in front of them and they basically lose all common sense. If it helps his case with you, he talked about you when he got drunk. Only to me, as far as I know, and never by name."

So Cav didn't walk away without remorse. Even though it shouldn't, the regret and sadness she just described make me feel a little better. Like I mattered.

"Enough, Win. You good on the lines now?"

My gaze darts from Cav back to the blonde, following the change in subject like a tennis ball across the Wimbledon court.

"They should know better than to pull this crap. I forget the lines as soon as we wrap. It's the only way I can make room for new material."

"It's *Casablanca*. It's not complicated."

"*Casablanca*?" I ask, insinuating myself into the conversation.

Cav nods. "We just wrapped the filming of the remake. That's what we have to go into the studio to do the voice-overs for."

Windsor grabs an orange handbag off the table between two club chairs facing the desk. "As long as you can keep from breaking Peyton's face, we'll be all good."

Cav's expression darkens immediately. "Fucking punk. If he says a goddamn word to Greer, I will not be responsible for my actions."

"To me?" I'm so confused. How do I fit into this?

Windsor smiles triumphantly. "Cav has already defended your honor with his fists once on this set. Mitch will kill him if he does it again."

I look from one to the other. "Umm . . . details?"

Her laugh sounds exactly the same as it does on TV. Husky, sexy, and perfect. "Don't you worry about it. Just be happy you've got a real man and not some pussy-ass bitch."

Hearing the crass words come out of her mouth takes me aback, and she sees it on my face.

"I can tell it how it is. My ex-husband was way too much like Peyton for comfort." She tosses her golden locks. "So glad that's over. Can you even imagine what a bloodbath it would've been without the prenup?"

I can't imagine, nor do I want to. This entire conversation is so far outside of what I expected to be involved in when I woke up from my nap, I'm not sure how to react.

Windsor tucks her clutch under her arm and turns to Cav. "I'll see you tomorrow. Don't be late or Mitch will kill you. You should've heard him after you told him that you couldn't get back a couple days ago. Pretty sure his blood pressure is through the roof, so that whole relaxing vacation thing is shot."

Cav shrugged. "Some things are more important than work."

Windsor's gaze lands firmly on me. "I can see that. So nice to meet you, Greer. I'm sure I'll be seeing more of you." She doesn't slow, just clicks on her sky-high heels out the front door.

I turn back to Cav. "She's . . . interesting."

He smiles. "Windsor's a fireball. Not a firecracker, because it doesn't have enough destructive power."

It's on the tip of my tongue to ask him if they were . . . together, but I don't honestly want to know the answer. Can my newfound jealous streak handle knowing that he and the perfect blonde had a thing?

Who am I kidding? They definitely had a thing. The

red carpet pics of the two of them were snapped regularly for months.

My thoughts must be clear on my face, because Cav is studying me. "She's a good friend. That's all."

"I didn't—"

"You didn't have to. She was a great date to premieres because I didn't want to take someone who was going to expect more, and she was going through a nasty divorce. She's good people, and definitely a helpful friend to have in this business. Basically, she's Hollywood royalty. Born and raised in this business, so she was able to teach me the ins and outs and tell me who I could and couldn't piss off."

"And you actually listened to her?"

His chest shakes against my side before the deep chuckle hits my ears. "Sometimes. Not all the time."

"Who's this Peyton guy? Why'd you break his face?"

Cav's chuckle evaporates and he stills. "Not important."

I pull myself out from under his arm so I can face him. "That sounds like bullshit."

He sighs, looking to the ceiling before finally meeting my gaze. "That's how I found out about the ad. Little punk wanted to go apply in person. He's a piece of shit, and didn't understand how to keep his mouth shut after I told him he needed to forget reading it."

"So you shut it for him?"

A single nod.

"You're such a caveman."

A smirk tilts the corners of Cav's mouth. "Call it like you see it."

I don't have time to react as he ducks his shoulder and tosses me up and over it.

"Cav!"

"Just showing you how much of a caveman I can be, baby girl." He heads for the door and pauses in the entry-way. "Now where should I take you?"

His hand lands on my ass with a light *smack* just as my stomach growls too loudly for either of us to miss.

Cav turns away from the bedroom. "I guess that answers that. Time to feed my woman."

And that's how I get my first tour of Cav's house. Upside down and over his shoulder.

CHAPTER
NINETEEN

Cav

Having Greer sit on a bar stool in my sprawling kitchen, sipping a glass of Napa chardonnay while I peruse takeout menus and we debate dinner choices, is everything I've wanted for years.

I finally feel like I can offer her a life that's up to her standards. I'm so far removed from the guy who lived in a 400-square-foot studio apartment with more water stains on the ceiling than paint on the walls. Back in those days, I could read it in her eyes—*why doesn't he ask me to come home with him?* Because home was nothing I could be proud of, and I didn't want Greer to see me that way. Pride is a dangerous thing, but when it's all you've got, it's everything.

We decide on a whole spread of Thai food, and I make the call.

"Thirty minutes," I tell her, and Greer's stomach rumbles again. "You gonna make it?"

She takes another sip of her wine and nods. "Of course. Although, I can't promise not to be tipsy by the time it gets here." She lifts the almost-empty glass toward me, and I pick up the bottle and pour another measure in. "Empty stomach plus alcohol, and we know what can happen . . ."

"That's not always a bad thing." I like the idea of Greer tipsy enough to lose her inhibitions, but still together enough to know exactly what she's doing.

"I figured you'd say that."

I pour myself a Scotch, neat, and lift the glass. "Why's that?"

"Because you're already thinking about how you're going to fuck me tonight."

She doesn't mince words.

I tip back a sip of the Scotch. "You're not wrong."

"So, what's it going to be?" She lifts a dark eyebrow. "How do you want me, Cav?"

Tonight I don't want anything crazy. I just want to have her under me in my own bed, like I've imagined for years. It sounds too sentimental to say aloud, though.

"I guess you'll have to wait and see. First, food."

I'm falling in love with her again. It isn't the second time. Or the third. Or the fourth. With Greer, it seems to happen constantly. In Belize, it happened over margaritas and again over jellyfish stings, and tonight it's over pad thai and tom yum soup.

After we've stacked the leftover takeout containers in the fridge, I lead her into the media room. She may be expecting something depraved and wicked, but I want a normal night. The kind we never really got to have together. I bring up the movie menu and hand her the remote.

"Your choice, baby girl. What do you want to watch?"

Greer looks down at the remote and then back up at me. "Really? You're a guy handing over the remote? What do I owe you for this?"

"Hush." I press a kiss to her lips and walk her backward until she bumps into the edge of the plush gray leather sofa and plops down onto the cushion. "Any more sass and I'm taking your movie-picking privileges away."

Greer clutches the remote tight to her chest. "No way in hell. You can't take this back. It's not every day I get the chance to watch *your* movies with *you*."

I wince at her words. "You're not really going to pick something of mine, are you?"

Her little smirk is too cute not to kiss off her lips. When I pull away, she has an eyebrow raised. "I'll play fair. Which one did you imagine me watching? Which one did you want me to see? And don't you dare lie to me and tell me you didn't."

How does she cut right to the heart of me every time? It's like she has an uncanny knack for it. Or maybe I'm just that transparent.

I take the remote from her and flip through the movie listings, not even sure the one I'm looking for will be included. When I land on the title, Greer makes a grab for the remote but I hold it out of reach.

"No fair. I said *your* movie."

I press PLAY and the surround sound comes to life. "You wanted the one I thought most about you seeing. And that's what you're getting."

Greer looks at me, her features lit with the flashes of white coming from the huge screen. "You're not even in this movie. Isn't this a Bruce Pitt action flick?"

I tuck the remote into the side of the couch and wrap an arm around her shoulders to pull her against me. "Then I guess you're just going to have to watch really closely, because that flash of Bruce Pitt's ass in the last third of the movie? Not his. The kickass stunts through the entire thing? Not him."

Her face turns up to mine, shock imprinted on her features. "Women went crazy over seeing that glimpse of his ass! That was you?" Wonder coats her words.

"I'll pause it during the credits so you can get a good look at my name."

Greer's eyes widen further. "No. Way. That's crazy. This movie only came out like six months after you . . ."

She trails off, but I know what she was about to say . . . six months after I left New York. I might as well fill her in on my past and how I got started in the movie industry.

"It was my first stunt job. I showed up in Hollywood, fresh off a Greyhound, didn't know a soul. Got a room at an extended stay motel that doubled as a cheap place for hookers to turn tricks and crackheads to find a fix. It wasn't a good scene. I only had a few grand, and I knew it would go quick. I needed work and took a couple odd jobs working on sets. Manual labor, that kind of thing."

The opening credits of the movie start to roll, and Greer reaches over me to grab the remote and pause it. "Keep going. I want to hear this."

"Well, I got to talking to one of the stunt guys on set about gyms nearby that didn't charge an arm and a leg, and he asked me why the hell I was doing the fetch-and-carry when I could easily be working stunts if I wasn't afraid to break a few bones on occasion. Told me I had the right build for it."

"And then what?"

Greer's eagerness to hear the story of my past kept me talking. "We met up at the gym and worked out, and he told me he wouldn't be surprised that if I got into the stunt world, I'd also get asked to be a body double in some scenes. He hooked me up with his union, and that's how it started." I nod toward the movie paused on the screen. "So this was my first job. I didn't expect the body double part, but when Bruce got to that part in the filming, he said no way, he was too old to be flashing that shit around. I was already doing the stunts, and he dragged me in front of the director."

I close my eyes for a moment, picturing it, and add some grit to my voice as I repeat the words Bruce said to the director that day. "You want ass? Film his. My wife won't believe it's mine, but you work the angles right and the rest of the world will."

Greer's giggle erupts beside me. "No way! Are you serious?"

My own chuckle follows hers. "Yes, absolutely serious.

So that's how millions of women fell in love with my ass and didn't even know it was mine."

Greer leans over and buries her face in my neck. "They would've fallen in love with it even harder if they'd known it was connected to a guy who was younger and hotter than Bruce Pitt." Her hand snakes out and grabs the remote. The movie starts playing immediately. "Now, don't make me wait any longer. I've gotta see this ass."

I snatch it back from her purely because I'm proving a point. "You can see it anytime you want, baby girl. That ass is all yours."

Greer bites down on her lip and lets it slide through her teeth. "Is it truly mine?"

"I'm not letting you peg it, but yeah, baby, it's all yours."

"Peg?"

I shake my head. "Innocent girl. Watch the movie."

"I'll be googling that as soon as I get my phone back."

"You do that, baby. Now, watch."

Greer demands that I identify every moment I'm on-screen, and I comply. It might be the most fun I've had . . . ever. Even when she makes me replay the ass-flashing scene, in slow motion, *seven times*.

After the seventh time, she turns to me. "Okay, one more time."

"Greer." Her name comes out as a growl. I can only take looking at my ass so many times.

She holds up a hand. "Hear me out."

I sigh and wait for her to continue.

"You gotta stand up. And, you know . . . drop trou. I need to compare side by side."

"You've got to be joking."

She points to the very serious expression on her face. "Do I look like I'm joking, Hollywood?"

I pinch the bridge of my nose and shake my head. "Seriously?"

"Pleeeease."

Standing, I stare down at her. "Really?"

Greer nods her head so fast, she looks like the cutest and most excited bobblehead on the planet.

The things I would do for this woman.

"Fine, but it's not like you haven't seen my ass before." I turn my back to her and go for the button on my jeans.

"I know, but seriously, I can't miss this opportunity. I'd be thrown out of the female gender if I passed it up."

I glance over my shoulder at her. She's not looking at my face; that's for damn sure.

"Impossible."

"Come on, stop stalling. Oh, wait. Closer to the screen first."

Shaking my head and deciding that payback is going to be fun, I walk toward the screen and lower my pants so my ass is hanging out.

"Shirt, Cav."

With one hand, I pull up my shirt. "Woman, when I get my hands on—"

"Shhh. I'm appreciating this."

Several moments of silence follow before I crane my head around to see what she's doing. Greer stands and comes toward me, her eyes darting from the screen to my ass.

"Well, I'll be damned. That is the finest ass I've ever seen."

And before I know what she's going to do, she tosses something at it. I flinch when I feel the edge of something hit my right cheek.

"What the—" My eyes snap to Greer's.

She's ducking her head, her hand over her mouth to stifle her giggles. "I had to see if I could bounce a quarter off it."

"Where did you find . . ."

She jerks her head toward the couch. "Between the cushions. I took it as a sign."

I yank my pants back up and drop my shirt before turning and rushing her. Tackling Greer to the couch, I cover her with my body and silence her laughter with my lips. When I finally pull away, I stare into her dark gaze, sparkling with humor.

"I fucking love this, Greer."

Her eyes go wide and a small smile curves her lips. Both hands slap down on my ass, and she squeezes.

"I do too."

CHAPTER TWENTY

Greer

I've been dreading this call, but I know I can't keep putting it off. Creighton has to be losing his mind. I'm surprised there aren't already milk cartons with my picture on them, actually.

Do they even still do that? Who drinks milk from a carton anyway? Parents in Manhattan probably don't allow dairy in schools these days.

And once again, I'm trying to put off calling my brother. He's going to yell. I hate it when he yells. Especially when I know he's well within his rights to yell. Although, to be fair, I didn't kidnap *myself*. But it's not like I can use that as an excuse. He'd kill Cav. *But then he couldn't use Dom to bury the body.*

Stop.

I woman up and pick up Cav's house phone. I have

very few numbers memorized, but Creighton's is one of them.

I'm shocked when Creighton answers on the first ring, especially when he shouldn't recognize the number. Unless he does . . . because Cannon seems to know everything about everyone.

"Greer, is that you? Because if it's Westman, you better put my sister on the phone right the f—"

"It's me," I force out.

"Thank Christ. I've been losing my goddamned mind—and trying to keep this from Holly. She doesn't need this kind of stress right now."

Guilt doesn't trickle into me like it usually does at Creighton's comments. No, this time it's a flash flood.

"I'm sorry. I—"

Why didn't I come up with a plausible excuse before I dialed? Oh, that's right. I was worried about milk cartons. *Brilliant, Greer.*

Instead, I do what comes naturally when all little sisters deal with overbearing big brothers. I get defensive and a little bratty.

"You can't keep me locked up in some Podunk town with a security guard for a babysitter. That's not cool."

"I can do whatever the hell I want if it means keeping you safe."

"From Cav? Because he's the last person you need to protect me from." Even when he was keeping his identity from me, Cav's first priority was keeping me safe.

"He's a manipulative liar, Greer. You're too blind to see it. This isn't like the time you loaned two thousand dollars to the temp doorman because his mother needed surgery, and then he disappeared. It's not even like the time you offered up your credit card to cover your friends' bar tab that ended up costing me ten grand."

"Stop. That's enough." My voice is hard when I interrupt Creighton's warm-up of the litany of stupid or naive things I've done. "I get that I don't always make the best choices. I've done a lot of stupid things. But at some point, you've got to let me live my own life, Crey. I'm staying out of the press. I'm safe. And most importantly, I'm exactly where I want to be."

My brother is quiet on the other end, and I can imagine his eyes narrowed and jaw clenching so hard, his teeth grind together. I'm not afraid to stand up to him, and this time, it matters more than it ever has before.

I swallow, my grip on the phone turning sweaty as I wait.

"Are you staying in California?"

I release the breath I was holding. He's relenting. Well, at least as much as Creighton ever relents.

"For a little while, at least."

"Say the word and I'll have a jet waiting on the tarmac for you—day or night."

"I'm not going to need it."

A long sigh comes through the phone, but the tail end sounds more like a growl. "You better not, because I don't care if I share blood with him. I will kill him if he hurts you."

His death threat brings a smile to my face. This is the brother who wants the best for me, even when he doesn't agree with what that is.

"No one's going down for murder in this family, Crey."

"I wouldn't get caught."

"I know you wouldn't."

And with that, we say our good-byes and hang up. I nod my head and speak to the empty office.

"That went better than expected."

Next, I lift the phone to dial Banner. She answers on the first ring.

"This better be my best bitch telling me what the hell happened to you!"

"It's me."

Banner sounds like she doesn't even take a breath. "I've been freaking out since you sent me that text. And the person who answered my reply *was not you.*"

"Crap. Sorry about that. I . . . after I got back to Holly's grandma's house, things sorta took an unexpected turn."

"Tell me everything. Now."

"Cav kidnapped me."

"Damn, that sounds hot. Was it hot?"

"Once I realized I wasn't going to be spending the rest of my reproductive life in a harem wearing a Princess Jasmine costume? And after I got over wanting to murder Cav?" I pause to consider. "Maybe a little."

"No shit. Adding to my sexual bucket list." Banner puts me on speaker, and I hear shuffling before the sound of scribbles.

"You have a sexual bucket list? And you keep it updated?" I'm not sure which surprises me more.

"Damn right I do. Goals only become real possibilities

once you write them down. I use the SMART goal meth-od. Specific, measurable, achievable, results-driven, and time-bound." Banner rattles it off so easily.

It's times like this when I remember my nut job of a best friend has crazy-smart scientists for parents who had her admitted to Mensa after her first qualifying IQ test. I think we were in elementary school. Crazy-smart runs in the family.

And this is just one more example of good intelli-gence being used for all the wrong reasons. Or maybe she's smarter than all of us.

"Have I told you lately that I love you?"

"No, but if you sing that song to me, I'm going to reach through this phone and bitch slap you."

I hum a few bars, and she interrupts.

"Has he fucked you on the Hollywood sign yet? Is he going to?"

"Oh my God, don't tell me that's on your list."

I press my ear closer to the phone to hear what sounds like the tapping of a pen on paper. "No, but I'll consider it. I think there's a trespassing issue."

I snort. "Says the girl who broke into the school to have pool sex during spring break when we were seven-teen."

"Unfair! There was tequila involved. I can't be held re-sponsible for my actions."

I recall the night I placed the ad. Tequila is a sneaky devil. "Fair enough. So tell me, what did Logan say when you texted him back? He's a super-cool guy."

Silence hangs on the line for several beats. "Super-cool

as in he needs a good personality to redeem him from being an overall-wearing country hick with a beer belly, or super-cool like he's a backwoods Ken doll?"

I'm used to Banner's random questions, so this one doesn't throw me much. "Definitely not a Ken doll. But not a GI Joe either. He'd be an action figure all his own. You can tell he hasn't been out of the military long. The buzz cut is grown out to shaggy, but he's got that posture you can't miss. Probably because he's like six three and his shoulders are as wide as Cav's."

"Sounds like he's a brick shithouse. What about his eyes? Is he stubbly? Does he wear all camo?"

Whoa. These aren't the kind of questions Banner would normally ask. "What exactly happened when you texted him back? Are you intrigued?"

"No, of course not. I just . . . Never mind."

Did her voice get a little breathy? "Banner? Is there something you need to tell me?"

"Oh shit, I just realized I have a project due by end of business today. I better get back to it. 'Bye, babe. Make sure to use lots of lube!"

Something isn't adding up here, but before I can question her further, the call has ended.

CHAPTER
TWENTY-ONE

Greer

I've never understood what it takes to make a movie, and now I'm in a recording studio listening to Cav and other actors recite their lines so the voices can be layered over part of the film where the mic went out.

Casablanca.

How did I not have any clue they were remaking the movie? A classic, obviously, and not something I would have ever expected to see Cav in. But then again, he makes a perfect Rick. Windsor is gorgeous as Ilsa, and then there's Peyton DeLong, who I hate on sight, even though I thought he was cute in his last romcom. If Cav determined his face needed smashing because he was talking shit about me, I don't ever need to meet him.

But Peyton's done with Victor Laszlo's lines first and comes out of the booth where they're recording.

I divert my attention to my nails, which suddenly become the most fascinating things on the planet. I'm staring down at them when feet enter my field of vision. Loafers, actually. The kind you see in Dolce & Gabbana ads but can't picture any red-blooded man actually wearing. Apparently Peyton DeLong isn't worried about being mistaken for a red-blooded man.

"You sick of your ride on his dick yet? Because I've got six inches waiting for you."

I choke on the words *six inches* and lift my head enough to stare directly at his belt buckle. Then I raise my eyes the rest of the way up to meet his.

"I'm sorry, I must have misheard you."

Does he really think it's acceptable to come over here and speak to me like that? I know I opened myself up to all sorts of nasty comments when I posted my ad, but you'd think a guy who's won so many Teen Choice Awards and statuettes for being a great role model for kids would have some class.

And you'd be wrong.

"That's all you care about, isn't it? Why is it you little rich girls always go for the trash before finding someone who's your social equal. We get sick of sloppy seconds, you know."

Oh. My. God. Is this guy for real? Cav is going to do more than just break his face.

"I would suggest you move along, Mr. DeLong. I think it's safe to say you never have to worry about my being sloppy seconds for you."

Even saying the words gives me the creeps. *Gross.* I

wouldn't go near this guy's dick for all the money in the world.

And then he touches me. Uninvited. Hand on my chin, tilting my face upward.

I slap it away, but it's too late. The soundstage door slams open.

"I told you to fucking stay away from her. You just couldn't do it, could you?"

Cav yanks Peyton's arm away from me and shoves his chest. The other man stumbles back across the room, falling into a chair.

"You touch me again, and I'll make sure they blackball you, Westman. You can't fucking push me around."

"I can and I will. Watch me, you little fuck. You put your hands on a woman, and every time they're gonna side with me."

I stand and move behind Cav, my hand pressing against his back. "Baby, it's okay. He tried to impress me by telling me he had six inches for me. I hope he was joking, because that's just sad now that I've had a real man."

My words are pitched low, but I project well enough for Peyton to hear them clearly.

"You little—"

Windsor, who I didn't realize had followed Cav out of the soundstage, bursts into laughter. "Six inches? God, Peyton, at least tack on a few extra if you're going to try to make it sound appetizing." Her laughter quiets for a moment and her next words are hushed. "Oh Lord, did you already artificially inflate your size? Because if you did, that is sad. My ex-husband can recommend some excellent penis pumps. Guaranteed to give you at least a little more length and girth to please the ladies. You want his number?"

If I were on the fence about Windsor before, I'm now firmly in her camp. She's da bomb.com.

Peyton's face goes from flushed red to enraged red when she drops the penis-pump line. It's safe to say he probably wouldn't call 911 if any of us were dying.

"Fuck all of you. I'm done. If Mitch needs anything else, you can tell him to suck my dick."

"All six inches of it?" I can't keep the question from my lips, and Peyton snarls as Cav and Windsor laugh.

He turns and storms out the door.

"I always figured he had little-dick syndrome. It explains so much." Windsor taps a finger against her brilliantly red lips. "I'm guessing he's a solid five inches. Maybe four. His poor little Disney Channel girlfriends. They're going to be in for quite the shock when they get a look at a real man."

Tears of mirth spill down my cheeks and I try to wipe them away discreetly, but it's impossible. Cav pulls me into a hug and uses his thumbs to catch them.

"It's not usually that eventful around here," he tells me, "but goddamn, Peyton's a fucking douche. Next thing you know, we'll be catching pics of him in some European gossip rag with a horse cock photoshopped on it so he can save face."

I press a hand to my chest, but the laughter won't stop. "Oh my God. If this is your job, it's the *best*."

"Oh, honey, you ain't seen nothing yet," Windsor

drawls like a perfect Southern belle. She looks pointedly at Cav and drops the accent. "You're bringing her to the party at my place tonight. It's a small gathering of friends, nothing too intimidating. The paps won't be able to get past the front gate, so you don't have to worry about that nonsense. It's going to be a hell of a good time. Only the fun people. None of the little pricks like Peyton."

Party? At Windsor Reed's Hollywood pad? Banner will kill me if I say no.

I look to Cav and he shrugs. "If you're up for it, we can go."

My mind instantly goes where every girl's mind goes at this point—what am I going to wear?

"Um, I didn't exactly come party-dress ready on this trip," I mumble to Windsor.

Her smile is wide and genuine. "No worries about that. I'll have something sent over. I wouldn't let you show up underdressed or out of place. Trust me, G."

All of a sudden, my world has tilted in an entirely new direction. With the nickname she's bestowed on me, the same one that my best friend uses, I feel like I've become part of Cav's world.

Is this what he wanted when he brought me here? To see if I could fit and we could have a life outside New York and both our pasts? Is that what I want?

A few weeks ago, I would have said my entire life was in New York—my job, my friends, my family. But right now, with Cav's hand resting on my hip, I feel like I really could have a new beginning here. Maybe a new job. More friends. And my own family. It's a foundation-rocking thought, but I'm thinking it nonetheless.

Windsor is waiting for an answer, and I give her the only one I want to speak. "That would be great. Thank you so much. I can't wait."

She smiles at both Cav and me. "You two are so fucking cute. Come have fun tonight; I swear it'll be worth it."

"Thanks, Win. We'll be there."

CHAPTER
TWENTY-TWO

Cav

"What the hell did she send you? Is that the whole dress?" I'm ready to kill Windsor.

Short. Tight. Red.

It's traffic-stopping.

In all reality, the dress is no worse than what you see any night of the week in the LA clubs, but on Greer, it looks sinful. I want to wrap her up in a nun's habit so no other man can see all her soft, creamy skin. Her dark hair is pulled up, leaving her neck bare and vulnerable.

"You don't like it?" Greer turns in the mirror, tugging the short skirt of the dress down so it covers a few inches past the curve of her ass.

"Fuck. I love it, but I still want to kill her. She knew exactly what she sent you, and she did it to see if I'd let you out of the house like that."

Greer turns, and her anxiety about the dress is clear on her face. I'm not helping matters with my outburst.

"It's not that bad, is it? I mean, it's not like you can see anything."

She's right, you can't, but the length of the dress and the color makes me want to bend her over and pull the skirt up before I paddle her ass until it matches the red of the fabric.

"You look beautiful, Greer. But I'm not going to be able to keep my hands off you while you're wearing it."

And dammit, she's my woman, so I don't have to keep my hands off her.

I think back to the games we played in Belize, and how hot they were for both of us. For me, there was no pretending. I like being in control, and Greer responded like she was born to it. But is she game to make it a permanent thing in our relationship?

"I wouldn't expect you to keep your hands off me."

Her flirty tone gives me the opening I need. "When we were in Belize, you let me take the lead. And if we were still there, pretending no rules applied, I'd tell you to take off your panties and hand them to me." I step closer to her. "What I need to know is how you'd react if I told you to do that here. Now. To let me take the lead again."

Greer bites her lip, her brain working overtime. I imagine she's flipping through the memories just like I am and trying to decide if she can take this chance with me.

What she says now will tell me whether she trusts me yet or not.

I open my mouth to tell her that there's no pressure,

she can think about it, but she beats me with her response.

"Yes. I want that."

"Are you sure?"

She stares up at me with those dark eyes, and I can read the excitement in them. "Yes, I'm positive."

"Then take off your panties and hand them to me."

Her pupils dilate at the order, and she slips into the role like a seasoned actress. "This dress is way too short for that. I'll end up flashing everyone when I get out of the car, and it'll be like that Britney debacle, but worse, because it'll be *me*."

I knew Greer was perfect before, but this just sealed it. I beat back the smile tugging at my mouth and see just how far she's willing to go.

"Then I guess you better keep your legs closed like a good little girl so no one sees that pussy. Because it's mine, and I'll spank your ass if you show it to another man."

"You can't be serious." She might sound like she's protesting, but without a bra, her nipples are pressing against the fabric of the bodice.

"You like it. Now, take those panties off and hand them over."

Greer is practically squirming where she stands in the black stiletto sandals Windsor sent along with the dress.

"If they aren't in my hand in ten seconds, you're going to be wearing a plug all night, and instead of enjoying the party, you're going to be focused on keeping your ass tight so it stays in."

Her dark eyes go wide. "You— What— I—" She stammers words that make no sense.

"Ten," I say, starting the count.

Greer stays still, arms by her side, her face the picture of shock.

"Nine." I hold out my hand. "Eight."

She doesn't move.

"Fuck, baby. My cock is going to be hard all night knowing your ass is filled. Seven."

Greer shifts into action, reaching up under the dress.

"Pull it up. I want to see that pretty pussy after you take them off."

She bites her lip but complies, drawing the skirt of the dress up to her waist and revealing a black lace thong.

"Did you get those panties all wet for me?"

Greer peels them down and steps out of them one leg at a time. "Maybe." Her response is a whisper.

I hold out my hand. "Bring them here. I want to see." When she doesn't step toward me, I continue my count-down. "Six."

Shuffling across the floor, her skirt around her waist, Greer comes to me and places the ball of lace in my hand. I lift it to my face.

"Naughty girl. Show me that tight little pussy. I want to see how wet it is."

Greer's pupils dilate further as she stares at me, ab-sorbing my command. She shifts to spread her legs, and I shake my head. "Turn around. Bend over. Spread your ass with both hands. I want to see everything, you dirty girl."

I squeeze the soaked lace in my fist, waiting and won-dering if she'll keep following my lead.

Her nipples bead up perfectly against the red fabric,

and I promise myself they'll be in my mouth tonight. I might even clamp them. I think she'd love it.

"Five." I continue my countdown.

"But—"

"Four. You want a plug up your ass? All you have to do is ask, baby."

Greer spins around on shaky heels, and I catch her elbow to steady her.

"Bend over. Don't make me tell you again."

She listens, bending forward until her ass juts toward me obscenely. But it's not obscene enough. I want it all from her.

"Now, reach back and spread your ass apart. I want to see it all. I want to see that pussy dripping down your legs."

Greer's sharp inhale of breath is the only sound in the room as she follows my orders and reaches back. Her hands pull her ass cheeks apart, showing me everything I want to see. Tight little asshole waiting to be fucked again. A dripping-wet pussy I can't wait to get my mouth on.

I reach out and slide two fingers through the slickness. *Jesus, she's soaked.* I pull my fingers back and step around her far enough to hold them up to her lips.

"Clean up the mess you made on my hand."

Her eyes dart up to mine, almost hidden by the shadow of her dark lashes.

"What?"

"You heard me. Suck my fingers clean."

When Greer's mouth drops open, I slide them between her lips. "Suck."

My dirty little girl follows orders, her tongue laving

Meghan March

every drop of her sweet juice.

"How do you taste, baby girl?" I ask as I pull my fingers free. "Do you like it?"

When she doesn't answer immediately, I tilt her chin up so I can see into her eyes.

"Give me words. I want to hear exactly how you feel about sucking your slick cream off my fingers."

She bites down on her lip, and I can't help but taunt her more. "If you don't give me words, I'll give you something else to keep your mouth busy, and then you can tell me how the taste of my cum compares to yours."

Greer sucks in an unsteady breath. "It's tart. Tangy. But not bad. Kind of . . . good."

My grin feels feral. "It's fucking delicious. You have the sweetest cunt I've ever tasted, and I think I'm overdue for a taste right now."

I move behind her, gripping both cheeks of her ass with my hands. "Keep them spread wide. If you let them slip, you'll get the plug, and you'll have to explain to Windsor why you're squirming under this tiny little dress."

CHAPTER

TWENTY-THREE

Greer

Oh. *My. God.* I've never been more turned on in my life.

When Cav asked if I wanted him to take the lead, it was like the scattered pieces of my brain snapped together. I loved having that before, and I want it again. No one has ever made me feel like he does. He has barely touched me, and I can feel the wetness sliding down the inside of my thighs. How does he do this to me? Only he can make me want all these dirty, filthy things. Not just once, but over and over and over.

When his tongue slides against my pussy from behind, I can't hold back the moan on my lips. I've been dying for him all day. Last night he took me in his bed, no toys, just straight vanilla sex. Or at least, that's what I think it would be called. It was amazing; I came twice before I passed out in his arms. But that isn't quite the same as this dark edge of pleasure we both clearly crave.

Now I understand the true meaning of "eating pussy" because Cav is voracious, leaving no spot untouched. My clit is aching with need, and my orgasm isn't far out of reach. When he slides his tongue back and licks me *there*, I jump and my hands slip, almost letting go of the grip on my ass.

Cav feels me start and slaps my hip. "Don't let go, baby girl, or I'll do more than put my tongue up this sweet little hole."

Tremors work through me. How can he say such dirty, filthy things, and why do I love them? I'm soaked, quite literally dripping, and he's giving me no mercy. When he reaches around to pinch my clit between two fingers, I completely lose it. My orgasm slams into me and my scream fills the room.

Waves rush over me again and again, the aftershocks ricocheting down my arms and legs. I never want to let go of this feeling. I love it. And I'm dangerously close to admitting that I love him.

"If I were a nice guy, I'd let you come again for me, eat you until you scream some more."

Cav stops speaking to do exactly what he says—lick and suck and nip at my pussy and my ass until another orgasm is building just out of reach. And then he stops abruptly and pulls away.

"But I'm not that nice. I want you wet and aching for me all night. I want you thinking about what I'm going to do to you when I get you alone. How deep you're going to take my cock down your throat. How hard I'm going to fuck you. How it's going to feel to have your pussy and your ass filled."

Just his words send punches of lust through me.

"But I want—"

Cav pulls my hands away from my ass and forces me to stand. "And you're going to get it all." After spinning me around, he pulls my skirt down. "But when I say."

I'm stunned and shaking on borrowed heels, in a borrowed dress, with a body that's dying for the man standing before me.

"Oh, baby, you look beautiful. Those cheeks are flushed." He skims the back of his fingers over my burning face. "These nipples are so fucking hard." He lowers his hand to stroke them as I arch into him.

Finally, he rubs his hand over my pussy, pressing lightly against my clit. "This pussy is going to stay wet for me all night until I'm ready to fuck it. Isn't it?"

At this rate, I'm going to be wet and waiting for him for the rest of my damn life.

"Tell me."

"Yes," I whisper, wanting to taunt him the same way he's taunting me. "I'm going to be wet all night, constantly thinking about how hard I'm going to get you with my mouth before you bend me over and fuck me, and about how good it's going to feel when you fill me up."

His eyes flash golden-green. "You're goddamn perfect, Greer. That filthy little mouth of yours is going to get you fucked like the dirty girl you are."

I bite my lip because the only words on my tongue are

more pleas that he not wait and take me *right now*. But I can read the look in his eyes. This is his game. He's going to tease me all night until I can't take it anymore. It's a game I'm ready to play.

"I can't wait," I tell him. Lifting up on my toes, I press my lips to his jaw.

Cav's eyes heat. He wants me just as badly as I want him.

Tonight's going to be fun.

CHAPTER TWENTY-FOUR

Greer

I'm no stranger to high-society parties, but that doesn't mean I'm ready for glitz and glam at Hollywood levels. From the moment we're admitted behind the massive fence protecting Windsor Reed's home from paparazzi and curious onlookers, it's very clear this society girl isn't in New York anymore. It's not the money factor; it's the boldness of it.

Inside the gates, it seems there are no boundaries. Dresses barely cover the essentials, and I'm pretty sure I've already seen flashes of two women's lady bits before we're even out of the car.

Luckily for me, my man doesn't want me putting on the same show, so he lifts me down from the back of the SUV.

He nods to the driver. "I'll call you in a few hours."

"Yes, sir."

When our ride is gone, we walk up to the front door of a sprawling house with a similar Spanish style as Cav's, but where his is simple and understated, this house is over the top in every way, starting with the fountain in the front courtyard where two women are calf-deep and splashing water at each other. Two men, most likely their dates, stand back and enjoy the show. One of the women is wearing a solid white dress that the water has turned sheer. The bulge below the belt of one onlooker also can't be missed.

What kind of party is Cav taking me to?

One of the men lifts his chin to Cav, and he returns the gesture. The man's gaze lands on me and rakes down my dress so boldly, I imagine I can feel the trail. Cav's arm is already around me, but he splays his hand out on the front of my hip, his fingers edging toward my center, and squeezes me against his side.

It's a move of possession.

The other man's gaze falls away, returning to the show in the fountain. It's not until we're at the massive white arched front door that I recognize the man from the movie Cav and I watched the other night.

"Was that—" I start to ask, not remembering the guy's name.

"Yes. And he's got a thing for brunettes who aren't his, so watch yourself. If we get separated, find me or Windsor. Some of these guys are too helpful for the wrong reasons. Throw on a layer of entitlement and a coating of being really fucking impressed with themselves, you're more than likely to kick someone in the balls if they try to pick you up."

Instantly, I'm on guard. "Why would we get separated?"

Cav looks at me, not so far down as usual due to the borrowed heels I'm wearing, and clearly reads the uneasiness on my face. "I'm not planning on it, but I'm just saying, if we do . . . I want you to be prepared. There's no one here you can't put in their place with a few well-chosen words."

And with that little pep talk, Cav shoves open the wood-and-glass monstrosity that Windsor calls a door, and we step inside my first Hollywood party.

It's an odd sensation, seeing people and recognizing them, but never having met them before. Still, when nearly everyone in the room has been on TV, that's what you get. People are dressed in various levels of sophistication. Some eschewed the fancy vibe of the party altogether and wore jeans—or at least parts and pieces of them.

I'm scanning the room—taking in the former child star, the Oscar winner, the chart-topping pop diva, several TV personalities, and other generally famous people—when I realize something shocking.

They're all staring at us.

After a few beats, the novelty must wear off because their focus turns back to their conversational partners and drinks.

I look to Cav only to find a hard and forbidding expression on his face. A *don't fuck with me, I'm in the mood to hand you your ass* expression.

"Everything okay?" I whisper.

"We're good." He doesn't elaborate on why it was necessary to scare off everyone who dared look in our direction.

"You sure?"

I'm about to ask whether he's sure this party is a good idea when Windsor comes striding toward us on heels even taller than the ones she lent me. Given that she's at least five six without them, the heels put her close to six feet. She looks like a blond Amazonian goddess.

"You made it! Oh my God, that dress looks so much better on you than it did on my sister. I hope you don't mind that it wasn't one of mine, because I thought this one was the absolute perfect thing." Her gaze cuts to Cav. "Looking handsome yourself, but not nearly as foxy as your lady."

Cav's arm, still curled around me, squeezes instinctively. "That's as true a statement as I've ever heard."

Finding my manners, I say, "Thank you so much for the dress and the shoes."

Windsor tilts her head to one side and reminds me so much of my best friend, I feel the need to call Banner right that moment. I miss her.

"I bet he threw a fit when he first saw you in it and then decided to play barbarian all night, just short of stamping his name on your forehead."

I can't help but laugh because she hit that one right on the head.

"Something like that."

Windsor winks at me before glancing at Cav. "Exactly like that, I bet."

"That's enough out of you. We're here, she's not tossed over my shoulder, so count yourself lucky."

With a small, feminine shrug, Windsor laughs off his remark and gives us a rundown of the party. "I think everyone I invited decided to tell a friend, so things have gotten a little more out of hand than I'd planned, but I'm not all that surprised. You know how these things go."

She's clearly addressing that part to Cav, because I have zero idea *how these things go.*

"Food is set up in the dining room. There's the usual smattering of hors d'oeuvres, so help yourselves." She turns to me. "If you eat, you'll probably be the only female seen putting anything besides alcohol or a dick in her mouth, but it'd be a nice change of pace."

My gaze cuts to Cav and a smile plays on his lips. *She's for real. These Hollywood people are nuts.*

"Uh, okay. Maybe I'll break the mold." After all, Cav and I didn't exactly stop for food on the way here. And if I do nothing but drink on an empty stomach, I'm going to be awesomely tipsy really, really fast.

"Do that. You look stunning, and maybe some of these stick figures would get a clue that a real man wants a woman he's not afraid to break." She pauses for a second, as though considering whether to continue. "And if you have sex in any of the bedrooms, double-check the lock. You know I really don't want my house to be a breeding ground for sex tapes again."

Again? My brain is spiraling, trying to keep up with Windsor, my gaze once again darting between her and Cav. I'm waiting for Cav's response, but a man approaches

Windsor, and it takes me a moment to realize it's a guy from a movie I saw last summer.

"Baby, you've gotta give me another chance."

That's when it clicks. This is Windsor's ex that she's so happy to have out of her life. Apparently, she should have asked for his key back.

Or maybe that's not how these things work. Hollywood is a different universe, and no one gave me an interloper's guide to navigating it.

Windsor draws her spine straight and squares her shoulders. "Sean, that's never going to happen."

Cav releases my arm and steps beside her. "I think it's time you leave, man, because you clearly weren't invited."

"Fuck off, Westman. You can't be her guard dog forever." The man, Sean, flicks his gaze from Cav to Windsor to me. "Besides, looks like you've got a woman of your own finally. Maybe I should take her from you and see how you like it."

He's reaching out a hand toward me when Cav wraps his arm around my waist. "That's a bullshit statement and you know it."

"Bullshit or not, it sounds fair to me." The man's hand hangs in midair, waiting for me to shake it. "I'm Sean France—"

"He's a douche who couldn't keep his pants zipped around twenty-year-old girls the entire time we were married," Windsor interrupts. "And she's just a touch too old to be part of your target demographic, Sean. Move on, or I'm pretty sure you're going to be needing another rhinoplasty after Cav is finished with you. Leave now before I have security toss you out and this gets embarrassing."

In the face of so many threats, it would take a real man to stand his ground, but Sean France glares at all of us and walks away.

"He's not on your list. How the hell did he get through the door?" Cav asks.

Windsor shrugs, her attention following the man's movements. She clucks her tongue and we all turn. "Probably with her."

Sean stops at the side of a stick figure of a girl who looks like she's not quite old enough to drink despite the tiny dress, perfectly styled hair, and smoky eye makeup. Without a word, he grabs her hand and drags her toward the door.

"He really is a douchebag," I say, not even conscious I'm speaking the words until both Cav and Windsor turn to me.

"He really is," Windsor agrees, following the couple's progress to the front door. "And good riddance to them both. She's too young and stupid to realize that she's going to be too old for him to find sexy in about six months. He's got this weird slightly pedophile kink where he's always looking for the younger chick. It's creepy."

Sympathy for Windsor having been married to a guy like that wells up inside me. It doesn't matter who you are or how perfect your life seems from the outside, things can always be broken and fucked up on the inside.

"Enough of that downer. I'm going to make the rounds and check that everyone is having a wonderful time, alert security so Sean doesn't get back in regardless of who he has with him, and find myself a distraction for the evening. You kids have fun. Don't do anything I wouldn't do." She smiles at us and strides away with a little backward wave.

"Is she okay?" I ask Cav.

He's watching Windsor walk away, her laughter already ringing out, a little too bright and cheerful.

"She's a trouper. She and Sean have been split for a long time, but the guy can't seem to stay out of her face. It's not even that he wants her back, honestly. I think he just misses having the security of her covering for him and the ease of having someone else run his life. It's unusual for these Hollywood marriages not to be straight fucked up."

"Is that why you didn't run out and marry the first famous chick who fell for you?" My question is a quip, off the cuff.

Cav's eyes, looking steel-gray against his gray dress shirt tonight, cut to mine. "You already know the answer to that." When I don't respond immediately, he closes both his hands over mine and pulls our arms out wide until our bodies press together. "I was hung up on one particular woman, and she wasn't in Hollywood. Nothing here could compare to the hold you've had on me from day one, Greer. You still don't get it."

Cav's words are serious and completely at odds with the high-pitched laughter and conversation going on around us.

I don't know what to say, but I'm wishing we were anywhere but in the middle of Windsor's palatial home. I want to be back at his place, watching another movie without this crowd around us. Maybe pausing in the middle so he can bend me over the back of the couch and assuage the ache that continues to build inside me. Just the thought has me pressing my legs tightly together.

As usual, Cav doesn't miss a thing. "Aw, my baby girl still feeling the edge?"

I lean close. "You know you left me hanging. That was plain mean."

His eyes darken. "Don't think I'll leave you hanging for long. Now, let's make an attempt at being sociable so you can get the full experience, and then I'll take care of you."

The *I'll take care of you* is the only part of that sentence my greedy body cares about. I should probably be more intrigued by the famous people tipping back drinks, uncaring who sees them acting ridiculous.

We've only gone a few feet when it hits me—this is their safe zone. Windsor's house is their haven. No one is going to out them for acting that way here, I assume, within reason, so this is the place they let it all hang out.

It makes a certain sort of sense. Back in New York, there are certainly parties where I've felt the same way. When all the guests are part of a similar social and economic stratosphere, things get a little wilder than normal.

Windsor's home is a large square, with a mammoth courtyard in the center dominated by a sparkling blue pool, a hot tub, and several seating areas. A young couple is in the pool, and the woman has the man pressed up against the corner. Both of them are still fully clothed but completely soaked. In the hot tub, several women cluster around an older gentleman who I don't recognize as being in any films. But given the harem he's attracted and how they're pawing over him, he must be someone of note.

"Who's that?" I ask quietly, and Cav follows my line of sight.

"One of the top studio producers. Those girls are all B- and C-list actresses hoping to hop up on the A-train, and they know he gets a major say in casting all of the movies for a certain hot director."

"Is that normal?"

"For that particular producer and director, it is. They've been working together for twenty years, so it's a pretty well-known fact at this point." Cav turns us away as a woman climbs on the man's lap like she's about to ride him. "And he's fresh out of a divorce, so they're looking to take advantage of it."

In my opinion, it's the older man taking advantage of the younger women, but I guess my instincts are screwed up here. Maybe it's the women who are the predators in this situation. Everyone has a motive. It's really not all that different from New York.

We go back into the house through another open door, and I fall more in love with Windsor's place with every step. Yes, it's way too big for one person, but it gives off this airy vibe of being on a constant vacation. I love it. It's so different from my apartment and the street noise that I can't escape, even way up in my ivory tower. I know I'm lucky to not be living in a shoebox-sized place in the city, but even the most expensive penthouses in New York can't come close to competing with this.

Cav leads me into the dining room and the decadent spread of food along a buffet. It's virtually untouched, which surprises me more than I let on. Even if the stick-thin women are going to turn their *I'll just have a wheat-grass smoothie* noses up at this, why aren't the men eating?

A quick survey of the room shows that the lines at the bar service are dominated by men, so apparently they're all more worried about drinking than eating.

Cav has no such reservations. He grabs two plates and hands me one. "You're not drinking on an empty stomach."

"I'm going to be the only female eating in this entire place."

Cav shrugs. "Fuck 'em, Greer. You don't need to impress anyone. You're already the most beautiful woman here. The guys can't keep their eyes off you, and if I make it out of here tonight without putting my fist through someone's face, I'll count myself lucky." He reaches for the first set of tongs. "Eat, woman."

"Fine."

The choices are decadent enough to rival one of Creighton's parties. I stick to the veggies and seafood, and Cav loads up on meats and cheese. He grabs us both a drink before we set up at one of the tall tables lining the side of the room. They're all empty except for ours.

Cav doesn't seem to care at all, though. He digs into his plate with gusto. I've honestly never seen a man eat so much or so often as he does, but it explains why most of the guys I know don't look anything like him. I assume it takes a lot of protein to keep his physique intact.

It's almost laughable now when I think of Tristan. Tristan who could wear skinny jeans and be in no danger of sporting a dick print. I can't even imagine Cav trying to get them on. He'd probably bust the legs wide open. And for sure, there'd be no room for the equipment he's packing.

Speaking of his equipment . . . my gaze dips below his belt as he digs into his food.

"Eyes up here. You're not getting the D until I'm ready to give it to you."

My gaze snaps up to his. "How do you even know what I was thinking? I could've just been admiring . . . the fine craftsmanship of your belt."

"Stole it from costume off a set. And we both know you're full of it."

I roll my eyes and grab a shrimp off my plate. "I'm not full of anything right now, if you'll recall."

Cav waits until I'm done chewing my food before he leans close and speaks low into my ear. "You're gonna be full of something as soon as we finish eating."

His words have an immediate physical effect on me, and now everyone at this fancy Hollywood party is going to get a phenomenal view of my hard nipples.

Before I can reply, another man stops by the table. I cross one arm over my chest in what I hope is a casual rather than defensive-looking posture.

"Where the hell have you been, man? Been trying to track you down for poker night for weeks. It's like you fell off the damn planet."

The man is probably an inch taller than Cav, and is

as light as my man is dark. Sun-bleached blond hair gives the guy the look of a surfer. I can't recall his name, but Cav clearly knows him well because they do that half-hand-shake, half-backslapping hug that must be encoded in male DNA.

"Bohannon, good to see you, man."

Ah, that's right. His name is Silas Bohannon, and I remember him as a surfer because that's what he was in his last big movie.

"You gonna introduce me to this gorgeous woman?" he says, his aqua eyes on me.

"Not sure I should. You're a little too smooth with the ladies."

From his easy manner with Silas, Cav clearly isn't worried, but still the words give me a hint that this very attractive man has no trouble finding female company.

"She's safe from me. I've got my eye on a spitfire I haven't been able to pin down."

Silas's attention drifts, and I follow his line of sight as it lands squarely on Windsor.

Hmm. Interesting. I can't imagine she'd be stubborn enough to say no to this much man in her life . . . especially now that I've gotten an up close and personal look at pedophile Sean.

"Bo, this is Greer. Greer, Bo."

I shake his hand, but it's clear his mind isn't on meeting me, despite being personable and polite. Cav notices his distraction as well.

"Persistence, Bo. She's gonna give you a hell of a fight. You know she doesn't want anything to do with another guy from this world."

"She's fucking wrong if she thinks we're all like limp-dick Sean."

I toss in my two cents without thought or invitation. "I might be overstepping here, but sometimes a woman just needs to know what it's like to have a real man in her life. Especially if all she's ever known is the limp-dicked variety. Don't ask permission. Don't apologize. Just man up and go after what you want."

Both Cav and Bo's heads swing around to me in surprise, and honestly, I'm a little shocked by the words coming out of my mouth. Before Cav, I would have never said something like that. I guess that's proof of the changes he has brought into my life.

"A real man, huh?" Bo glances from me to Cav. "You sound like you're speaking from experience."

"Maybe," I admit.

Cav wraps his arm around my shoulders. "She knows exactly what she's talking about. Her advice isn't bad, but we both know Win won't be easily persuaded. Have you ever thought about kidnapping?"

I elbow Cav in the ribs, and he coughs when I make contact.

"Don't listen to him. She'd be a hundred times more likely to shank you than screw you if you kidnap her."

Bo's eyes narrow, and he looks from me to Cav. "Do I even want to know?"

I shake my head. "Just put that option out of your mind. I promise you, it's best for your continued long-term health."

Silence falls over the three of us until Bo speaks again. "What about tossing her over my shoulder and carrying her out so I've finally got her attention?"

I purse my lips and consider, wondering if the perfectly coifed Windsor would freak. She seems pretty damn cool, but you never know how someone is going to react to being manhandled. Who knew I'd freaking love it?

"You can give it a try."

Cav adds his opinion. "I say go for it. Greer's right—Win doesn't know what it's like not be in control twenty-four/seven. She might actually respond well to that."

Bo's mouth turns up in a sly smile. "I get the same vibe. I'll let you know how it goes." He nods to me. "Good to meet you, Greer. I trust you'll keep this guy in line."

"I'll do my best."

And then Bo is gone, heading in Windsor's direction.

"Is she ready for what's coming her way?"

Cav shakes his head. "No. Win's been living in her own little world for too long now. It's time she rejoins the rest of us in the real world. But Bo's got his work cut out for him. She's as resistant as any woman I've ever met to the idea of getting into another relationship. That's why it was so easy for us to be friends."

I want to ask the obvious question—*You really didn't sleep with her?*—but I keep it locked down. There's nothing to be gained by asking. If he did, it's going to ruin my mood, and it's kind of unfair of me to judge because I was sleeping with Tristan, but Cav doesn't hold that against me. And secondly, I like Win, and I don't want to feel an urge to claw her eyes out the next time I'm within two feet of her.

Yep, the newfound cray-cray jealous streak is still alive and well. Some questions are best left unasked.

Cav and I finish eating, talking to a few more people who wander by the table. So far, I've met more famous people in the last hour than in my entire life. My brother might be well connected, but that doesn't mean I get to rub elbows with most of his connections. Besides, investment bankers and industry titans aren't quite the same as larger-than-life film stars.

The best part about tonight? I'm learning a lot about Cav from these interactions. He's well liked, humbler than most, and seems very proud to have me on his arm. I don't talk much, mostly saying what I think is the right thing when it's my turn.

Cav and I leave the table after speaking with a director I think he'd like to work with—gleaned from my mad observational skills. He leads me back outside to the pool area and sits on a chaise lounge before pulling me down beside him. My third glass of red is going down just as smoothly as the last two, and I'm hoping I can discreetly ask Windsor what this incredible vintage is.

Cav is also on his third drink. I can smell the Scotch on his lips when he tucks his arm around my hips and leans down to ghost them over mine.

"You fit in here."

His words are a boost of confidence I didn't know I needed. I've been telling myself all night that these people aren't that different from me. I face many of the same challenges without having the same job. And I could probably buy and sell several of them, so there's that.

"I'm glad you think so." I pause, considering whether it's actually the compliment I took it as. "That's a good thing, right?"

Cav looks down at me, his brow furrowed. "Of course. Why wouldn't it be?"

I shrug. "It's clear you don't like all of these people, so I guess I wanted to make sure."

He considers before responding. "Do you like all the people in your crowd in New York?"

"Of course not."

"But would it matter to you that I fit in with them?"

"Yes and no. I don't care whether *I* fit in with them all the time, and they can be pretentious as hell."

Cav scans the room. "I feel the same way about the people here. There are plenty I'd rather avoid, a few I really like, and the rest I can either take or leave. What I was trying to say is I'm glad you don't feel out of place. This isn't the easiest crowd to work, but I never doubted you'd be able to handle it."

Again, his words fill me with warmth. When did it become so important to me to fit into his world?

When you decided you couldn't stand the thought of letting him go. The voice in my head doesn't let me get away with too much bullshit.

I drain the rest of my wineglass and set it on the glass-topped side table next to the chaise lounge and stand.

"I need to find the ladies' room."

Cav rises beside me. "I'll lead the way."

I'm tipsier than I expected, or maybe it's just the über-high heels, because I lean on Cav for support to keep me steady.

"You good?" he asks.

"I think so." The warm glow of a good buzz shimmers over my skin, putting me in a chill and happy mood.

Cav leads me around what seems like a quarter mile of hallways until he pushes open a door and flips on the lights. "I'll be outside."

I slip into the bathroom, which, like the rest of Windsor's home, is perfectly appointed. I'm washing my hands and admiring the cool fixtures when the door pops open and Cav steps inside and locks it behind him.

I meet his eyes in the mirror. "Knocking. It's a concept."

"You forget that I don't ask permission, baby girl."

That's when I notice the heat flaring in his gaze and his hand tucked into his pocket.

He pulls out a silky bag and holds it up. "Do you have any idea how hard it's been carrying this around all night and waiting for the perfect time to use it?"

"That's a hard question to answer when I don't know what it is."

"Bend over. I want your fingertips touching the mirror and your eyes on mine the whole time."

My body responds on command as my nipples harden against the bodice of my dress. All night, I've been acutely aware of the ache he left and his promises about later. Not to mention how careful I've been to keep my legs squeezed shut to prevent any accidental flashes of nakedness.

"Here? Now?"

Cav lays the bag on the countertop and smooths a palm up the outside of my leg.

"Wherever I want. Whenever I want. You going to argue with me?" He drags the very short skirt of my dress up, exposing my bare ass to the cool air.

I shake my head, my eyes never leaving his. "No. I've wanted it all night."

"Because you're my naughty girl. Can't get enough cock to keep you sated. Now I'm going to fill you up all the way."

I want to know what's in the bag, but I'm not going to ask because I know it'll just slow down whatever he's going to give me, and I refuse to take the chance.

"You liked when I tongued this tight little asshole, didn't you?" Cav's fingers trail across my ass and slip lower, pressing against the forbidden spot in question.

"Yes, you know I did." My reply is shameless, and I don't care.

"Such a filthy girl. You're gonna get a little filthier right here. I hope you can keep quiet, otherwise we'll attract an audience."

It's on my tongue to ask him what he's going to do to me, but again, I don't want to slow him down.

"I want to fuck that perfect ass again soon, so I need to get you ready for it."

My inner muscles clench at his words.

I should be horrified that he's going to do this here and now, while a good chunk of Hollywood's movers and shakers are outside this door, but for some reason that knowledge just ratchets up the excitement thrumming through me.

Cav's hand slides between my thighs.

"Fucking soaked, baby girl. You want this as bad as I want to give it to you."

My only response is a nod because his clever fingers are circling my clit and teasing me. I thrust my ass out further, uncaring whether it's obscene.

Cav removes his hand, but before I can protest, he shakes out the contents of the bag. I've seen one before, but never up close and about to be used on me—a shiny silver butt plug. It looks like it's metal, which is strange because I thought they were all silicone or rubber. And beside the butt plug in his hand is a single packet of what I assume is lube.

"I'm gonna fuck this sweet pussy while I've got your ass full of this little plug."

I want it. All of it.

Cav doesn't ask for my approval; he can see it in my eyes.

"Pull the top of your dress down, I want your tits out while I take you. You're going to watch me in the mirror, watch my face and see how much I love being inside you."

I move my hands away from where they've been touching the mirror at his earlier command and pull down the front of my dress. My breasts spill free, landing on the cool granite. The sensation of cold against hot has my body thrumming in anticipation as Cav coats the plug with lube and drizzles the thick, sticky substance on my ass.

"You're never going to want me to fuck you without

your ass full after this. Your little pussy is already so tight, I'm barely going to fit, and you're going to love it."

"Hurry," is all I can say as I slide my fingertips around my nipples, teasing myself.

"I'm calling the shots here." He presses the end of the plug against my tight muscle. "Isn't that right?"

"Yes."

"Yes, *sir.*"

I bite my lip at the burst of heat his command unleashes inside me. We've been headed down this BDSM road since the first time we were together, and if I needed any more confirmation, Cav's request is it.

"Yes, sir," I repeat.

"Now, press against the plug, I want to watch it slide in."

I do as he says, the cold metal sending chills skittering across my skin as it slips in. Biting my lip to contain the moan, I embrace the stretch and the pleasure that comes with it. When the base of the plug is seated against my ass, I release the breath I was holding.

"Fucking perfect." He pushes a hand between my thighs and groans. "You're soaked, baby. So fucking wet. You dying for me yet?"

"Please." I'm not ashamed to beg. I just want him.

Cav's fingers disappear, but the sound of his belt and zipper keep me from moaning another plea. He fits the head of his cock against my entrance and meets my eyes in the mirror.

He starts to slide in, his gaze intense. "Inch by inch, baby girl. You're taking all of it."

I suck in a breath because he's right. I've never felt so full as I do with the plug in my ass and Cav's cock thrusting inside me.

"Most beautiful woman I've ever seen, and you're mine. Every single fucking piece of you is mine. I won't take anything less, Greer. All of you. That's what I want."

He already has what he wants, but words are beyond me. All I can do is nod as he bottoms out and presses the plug further in.

"Oh my God," I murmur, the words coming out on a harsh breath. "Oh my God."

Heat burns in Cav's gaze as he flexes his hips again, driving the sensation higher. One touch on my clit and an orgasm would be imminent.

When Cav pulls back and plunges inside, I can read the pleasure on his face too. We're not going to last long.

And then he decides to prove me wrong.

Over and over, he powers into me, hitting my G-spot with each thrust. My orgasm hangs just out of reach until he wraps an arm around me and presses down on my clit.

"Brace yourself."

Slapping my hands to the countertop, I never break eye contact as he pounds into me again and again, the pressure on my clit shattering my control. The orgasm bursts from me, along with a scream I can't rein in. I don't care if someone walks in and sees us, because the orgasm is rolling forward with the force of a freight train, the pleasure doubling and tripling with every moment.

"Oh my God." I moan, tears rolling down my face at the intensity of the pleasure. I've never felt anything like this before and it's almost too much, but Cav doesn't stop or slow.

"Fuck, baby. I'm coming."

Two more thrusts and my scream matches his groan. I slump forward on the counter, my head hanging forward until my forehead touches granite, breaking eye contact for the first time since I looked in the mirror and met his gaze.

My legs tremble as my knees threaten to give out.

Cav stays still, his cock still pulsing out his release inside me. His left palm slides up my back and turns my head to the side.

"You okay?"

I try to nod, but I'm too boneless to move.

"I'll clean you up. Give me a second."

Cav can have all the seconds he wants because I'm going to need to be carried out of here. Preferably out a back entrance so I don't have to see anyone who heard me scream when my orgasm stole my restraint.

The reality of what we've done hits me. "What if someone heard?"

"Then they'll be jealous as hell. Don't worry about it."

Cav pulls out and cleans us both up, but he doesn't remove the plug. When I point out his oversight, his lips quirk up on one side.

"Told you, that's staying in. We're not done yet."

My eyes go wide—I can see them in the mirror—and Cav's smile broadens.

"Just wait, baby. You think I made you scream this time? I've got plans for you."

CHAPTER
TWENTY-FIVE

Greer

We walk out of the bathroom, and it's clear that my hair has been arranged in the *just been fucked* school of hairstyling. I swear every single person in this house is looking at me and knows that I've still got a butt plug pushed up my ass.

"Can we hurry?" I whisper to Cav, feeling more self-conscious with every step.

He stops in the hallway and looks down at me. "What's wrong?"

"They're all going to know what we did."

Cav's smile is slow, and I'm tempted to wipe it off his face. "Baby girl, we aren't the first and we won't be the last people to use that bathroom for that specific purpose." He glances out toward the pool area where topless women and men in briefs are playing a game of volleyball. "Besides, everyone is on the fun edge of hammered right now, so what we're doing isn't on their radar. You're good."

For some reason, his words do make me feel a little less like I'm walking around with a scarlet letter sewn on my dress, but I'm still ready to leave—for more than one reason. I might have just had one of the most amazing orgasms of my life, but I'm still hovering on the edge, courtesy of the plug.

"Okay. I am ready to—"

"You can't possibly leave yet," Windsor calls as she slides through one of the glass doors that opens to the pool. Our words must have carried further than I thought. "Things are just starting to get fun."

Cav relays our regrets, and I barely hear him because I can't stop watching the man whose eyes are glued to Windsor. Silas Bohannon doesn't look like the kind of man to let her get away for long. If I had to place my bets, I'd say she won't be spending tonight alone.

Cav gives Windsor a hug and thanks her for the invite, and I do the same, picking up on the tail edge of their conversation.

"Thank you again for letting me borrow the dress and shoes. They're beautiful, and I'll get them back to you as soon as I've had the dress dry-cleaned."

Windsor waves a hand. "Don't bother. That dress looks a hundred times better on you than it does on my sister. Keep it. Consider both it and the shoes a gift."

I squeeze Cav's hand in my surprise. "Can I at least pay you for them? I—"

"Gift, darling. I don't want anything at all from you,

except maybe your promise that you're going to keep Cav happy. I've never seen him like this, and frankly, it's a good look on both of you."

"Deal."

Cav's hand squeezes mine in return, and it's a promise I hope I can keep.

CHAPTER
TWENTY-SIX

Cav

Greer has been quiet ever since Windsor told her to keep me happy. I know Greer well enough to guess her brain is turning that one over and over in her head. We have no clearly defined future. Every time we're together, it's somewhere removed from her normal life, so I can't imagine it seems real. Having her here, in my world, has made it very real for me.

I can see her staying here. Living in my house. Coming to parties and events with me. Making a life and building a future. But there's so much pulling her back to New York, I don't know if I can make this a reality or not. Greer's brother will be the biggest hurdle, but I'm willing to take on Creighton Karas to have her with me.

That's assuming she wants to be here. It's a different world for her, but she has blended into it so effortlessly.

She didn't stare wide-eyed at the people at the party. She held her own and talked to them like they were normal. Which they are, for the most part.

Greer is used to dealing with money and power and status, which makes her even more ideally suited for living in Hollywood and all the bullshit that comes with it most of the time. I couldn't have picked a woman more perfect for the life I'm living. I just have to figure out how to get her to stay.

But right now, I need to get her out of her head because the creases between her eyebrows tell me she's drawing in and worrying over everything rather than enjoying the moment.

If we were in my car, I'd have her spread her legs, pull up her skirt, and make her play with her pussy until she was on the edge of coming. I'd make her hold off until we got to the house and she could come with my cock buried deep inside her.

I glance at the driver, pleased that his eyes are firmly fixed on the road. Greer's already in the middle seat, leaning against me, so I pull her tighter to my side and slide my hand up her thigh and under her dress. The heat from between her legs is impossible to miss. I lean down and speak low, directly into her ear.

"Is it the plug keeping you wet for me, or are you thinking about everything I promised I'd do to you when we got home?"

Greer's eyes cut up to mine before looking meaningfully at the driver.

"Answer my question."

"Both." Her response comes out on a whisper.

"Are you ready for a cock up your ass? Last time, you took it like such a good girl."

She shifts against me, and I take advantage of her movement to run my thumb over her slick pussy lips.

I groan at how wet she is. "You couldn't be any more perfect, could you? Always wet for me, always ready to take my cock any way I want to give it to you. Win had it wrong; you don't have to do a damn thing to keep me happy. I'm the lucky bastard who wants to do everything I can to keep you happy." I pull my hand out from under her skirt and unbuckle her seat belt to draw her into my lap.

I've never wanted this kind of closeness with anyone, but with Greer, it seems I can't get her close enough. It's as if I know there's no way in hell I deserve to keep her, but that doesn't mean I won't do everything in my power to bind her to me anyway.

I see her in every part of my future, whether I deserve to have her there or not. If we were in Vegas, I'd drag her in front of an Elvis impersonator and get my ring on her finger as fast as I could. Is this how her brother felt when he pulled his Vegas wedding stunt?

Impossible. Because I've got three years of wanting tied up with this woman. Greer's it. She's the one. She's been the one since the first day she sat down and talked to me in the student café. I knew then I couldn't keep her, but now . . . now, things are different. Years stand between me and the sins of my past. I'm not the same man I was then. Now, I'd argue that while I may never be good enough for her, at least I can give her the kind of life she deserves.

"I love you, Greer."

The words come out, and even though they're not the first time I've spoken them, it feels like it.

Her hand, already anchored behind my neck to help her keep her balance on my lap, flexes.

"I meant it before and I mean it now. I want you in my life. Here. I'll do whatever you need to make it happen. I won't wait another three years. Hell, I don't want to wait three months, but I will. Move out here, live with me. *Be* with me."

I hadn't intended to have this conversation right this moment, but now that the words are out, I can't pull them back, nor do I want to.

Greer's face is lit by the streetlights outside, and her mouth has opened into a small *O*.

"Are you serious?"

"Absolutely. I know your life is in New York, but I think you'd be happy here. Make a new life, with me."

Her clever little brain is working overtime as she considers my proposition. "Move in with you . . . and find a job here?"

"Or don't find a job, whatever makes you happy."

She rolls her eyes at that. "Not having a job wouldn't make me happy."

"Then find a job. I don't care what it is as long as it makes you happy and you fall asleep every night in my arms."

"What about when you're filming on location and you're not here?"

"Find a job you can do from anywhere, and travel

with me."

She goes quiet for a few moments, considering. "Are you sure? This is what you really want?"

"This is everything I want."

She presses her lips to my chin. "Okay. Then we'll figure out how to make it work. It might take some time to transition, but . . . I want that too. I don't want to go back to only seeing you on TV and in magazines. I don't want you to be the guy I knew once, but missed my chance."

"Good, because I just want you to be mine, Greer. Every day."

"I already am."

Triumph barrels through me, even though she doesn't say the words I've been waiting to hear, but I'm not going to push for them.

"I love you so fucking much, Greer, and I'll do everything I can to prove this is the best decision you've ever made."

She wraps both arms around me and squeezes. "You don't have to do anything. I already know it is."

CHAPTER
TWENTY-SEVEN

Greer

Cav carries me into his house—or rather, what's going to be *our* house—as the driver pulls out of the drive-way. Was I shocked to hear him say those words again to me? *Yes.*

So shocked that I couldn't gather myself enough to say them back. But I will. For the first time in my life, I'm both diving in and holding back. There's a tiny voice in my head that worries it's all going to fall apart and Cav will leave me shattered one final time.

Now that I've had him like this, I don't know how I'd recover. He's worked himself into my life in such a way that I can't see my future without him. I won't let that voice win. I have to believe in him. In us.

Cav lowers me to my feet in the bedroom, saying nothing as he unzips the dress and lets it fall to the floor.

I'm naked beneath it, and he kneels to unbuckle the straps encircling my ankles. My feet scream with relief when I step out of the shoes, and I'm bare before him.

Wordlessly, he strips. I follow his fingers as he undoes each button, tossing the shirt away before he kicks off the shoes and unzips the slacks. Pushing both the pants and his boxer briefs to his feet, he steps free of them and stands before me naked.

Cav takes my hand and leads me to the bathroom and flips on the shower. Once steam fills the enclosure, he opens the door and I step inside. Cav is moments behind me, and his hands are everywhere.

Seeking. Touching. Worshipping.

He doesn't miss an inch as he washes me. My hair, my body, everything. Some part of my overactive imagination tells me we're washing the past away and starting again for the last and final time.

I silence any remaining doubts. There are no more secrets between us, and I'm leaping. I turn in his arms and meet his gaze.

"I love you."

The words are quiet, but Cav can feel the force behind them. He wraps both arms around me and crushes me against him. Happiness radiates from him, and I know I've chosen the perfect moment. A new beginning.

"I fucking love you, baby girl."

His lips find mine and my body ignites. His tongue teases and his hands are everywhere.

I haven't forgotten the one extra accessory I'm still wearing, or the heat igniting once more between my legs.

I want him. *There*. And I'm not afraid to ask for it.

"Are you going to fuck my ass like you've been promising?" I whisper the words, but they still echo in the tiled shower enclosure.

Cav's lips curve into a grin. "You know I'm never going to say no to that."

"Good, because I want it."

"Then that's exactly what you're going to get." He releases me from his hold and places a hand on the glass. "I'll be right back."

Cav pushes the door open, and a whoosh of cold air hits my skin. He's only gone a moment before he returns with one hand full. A bottle of lube and . . .

"A vibrator?" My eyes find his and the smile firmly fixed on his face.

"Trust me, you'll love it."

Excitement ricochets from wall to wall. One thing I can be certain of—sex with Cav will never be boring, and I don't have any complaints about that.

He presses a button on the vibrator, and I'm already wet and wanting. My screams are going to echo off the walls of this shower in a way neither of us will ever forget.

Cav lowers the toy to my pussy and the vibrations hit my clit instantly. Shifting, I squeeze my legs together instinctively.

"Spread your legs, baby." He lifts my hand from where it hangs clenched at my side and wraps it around the handle. "You're going to play with this sweet pussy and help me tease the hell out of you while I get this ass ready for me."

The combination of the vibrations and his filthy words has me ready for whatever he's going to do. I want it all. I circle my clit with the toy as Cav watches, his gaze heating with lust.

"Fuck, you're so beautiful." He reaches behind me and presses against the base of the plug. "And now you're all stretched out for my cock. Are you gonna take it like a good girl?"

Nodding, I bump the toy directly against my clit, and shivers of pleasure tear through me.

How is it possible that my orgasm is already building? He's barely touched me and I'm already dying to come.

Cav buries his hands in my dripping hair and takes my mouth, shifting and angling our lips for deeper access. The vibrator presses harder against me, and I groan into the kiss.

He pulls back, putting an inch between our lips. "Can't ever get enough of you, Greer."

"Good. I don't want you to."

"It'd be impossible." He releases his grip on my hair, and his hands skim down the wet skin of my shoulders to cup my breasts. "You're so fucking perfect. These tits." He squeezes before pinching my nipples between the thumb and index finger of each hand. He releases them and continues downward, pulling the vibe away so one hand can cup me between my legs. "This gorgeous pussy." And then finally, his palms trail around my hips to grip both cheeks of my ass. "This heart-stopping ass."

"Glad you like them." My words come out on a half laugh.

"You're so much more than that, but that doesn't mean I can't appreciate them like you deserve." Two fingers reach into the crease and press against the plug. "I think it's time this comes out."

With a quick tug, it comes free, and I feel empty. From the look in Cav's eyes, I know I won't feel that way for long.

His cock is hard, pressing into my belly. "How do you want me?"

"Any way I can have you."

The plug clinks against the tile as it lands on the floor. Cav's hand wraps around mine and the vibe. "We're going to play first."

He circles it around my clit, and my legs part instinctively. "Put one hand against the wall and keep this on your clit."

He lets go and I follow his orders, turning to press my free hand to the wall.

"I loved fucking you in front of that mirror, seeing your face as you came." The head of his cock nudges against the entrance to my pussy. "But since I can't see your face now, you're going to have to let me hear how it feels."

There's no pause before he thrusts, burying his cock inside me. I moan, arching my back.

"Keep that toy on your clit, baby. I want to hear you scream when you come on my cock."

Before he starts to thrust, I hear the pop of the cap of the lube and the thick, cool substance slides down my crack. Cav's thumb presses against me and penetrates.

Cock, vibe, and finger. I'm not going to last long.

He works me over in alternating strokes until my legs

shake and my moans turn to screams of pleasure as my orgasm slams into me. We both pause for only a moment before Cav pulls out and presses his cock against my back entrance.

"You're gonna come again for me, baby. Fill your pussy with that toy."

I slip it inside, the vibrations sending shock waves through me in the aftermath of my orgasm. Cav presses into me at the same time, the streaks of dark pleasure twisting together with the burn and stretch as his cock sinks inside.

I don't think I'll ever totally adjust to having his cock in my ass. It's always going to feel too full, and with the vibe inside me, it's an even tighter fit.

"Fuck yourself with it in opposition to my strokes. Can you do that for me, baby girl?"

I nod, and when he pulls back and fucks into me, I find the rhythm and match it perfectly opposite. I'm moaning, on the verge of a full-body climax. Every inch of my skin seems to shimmer with the intensity of what we're doing. In and out, vibe and cock. I've never felt anything this intense in my life.

I can't hold back the scream that comes with the orgasm. I drop the vibrator, my body writhing against Cav's.

"Fuck. I'm coming." He pulls me close, wrapping both arms around me as he presses his lips to my shoulder to muffle his roar.

Pulse after pulse, I feel his orgasm. We lean against the shower wall, arms braced for support, for long moments. When Cav finally pulls out, I'm limp, barely able to stand on my own. He washes us both again, and lifts me out of the shower before wrapping me with a towel.

"So fucking perfect," he whispers as he dries me off and carries me to bed. "I love you, Greer."

"I love you too," I mumble as I drift off to sleep.

CHAPTER TWENTY-EIGHT

Cav

The only thing I want to do is stay in this bed, wrapped around Greer, and shut the entire world out, but the nonstop buzzing of my cell phone makes that impossible.

Grabbing it off the side table, I frown at the display. It's Banner. I saved her number the night I texted myself from her phone in the bar before *Operation Snatch Greer*. She must have figured out a way to restore the texts if she's got my number back. I'm not all that surprised at her resourcefulness.

"Hello?"

"Jesus, I thought you'd never answer your damn phone, and Greer still doesn't have hers, and there's an epic shitstorm unrolling right now."

Fuck. What now?

"What's going on?"

Greer turns to face me, one arm wrapped around her pillow, her eyes still heavy with sleep.

"Greer's uncle's body was found this morning. Creighton's been taken in for questioning, and Greer needs to get the hell home right now."

Fuck.

"What's going on?" Greer asks through a yawn.

"We'll be there in five hours or less."

"You better be, because if Creighton thought Greer's shenanigans were fucking with his business, this is probably a shit show on a whole new level."

I can only imagine. *Jesus.*

"We'll be there. Thanks for the heads-up."

I hang up on Banner and turn to Greer.

"We've got a problem."

CHAPTER
TWENTY-NINE

Greer

I hear the words Cav is saying, but they can't be right. I *know* for a fact that Creighton didn't have a damn thing to do with our uncle's disappearance. But how do I tell Cav that his and Creighton's father probably did?

"Are you going to call Dom?" I ask.

Cav shakes his head. "I hadn't planned on it. Why?"

"Because he's going to know a hell of a lot more about this than either of us."

He studies me, clearly getting that I know more than I'm saying. "Just say it, Greer."

I bite down on the inside of my cheek, figuring out how to explain it. *Now is not the time to mince words.*

"This was Dom's gift to Creighton when everything went south with our uncle and he accused Creighton of all sorts of crap at a shareholder meeting. Dom was going to take care of it. It was never supposed to come to light or blow back on Crey."

Squeezing his eyes shut, Cav scrubs a hand over his face. "Fuck. I should've known."

By silent mutual agreement, Cav and I jump out of bed and shove stuff into our bags. I'm dressed and ready faster than I've ever been before. He's already called to get us a flight and a driver, who is minutes away.

"Holly has to be freaking the hell out, which can't be good for her or the baby."

He squeezes my hand as he carries our stuff to the front door. "She's going to be fine. Crey has the best lawyers money can buy, and you know this won't stick."

"But what about Dom?"

Cav doesn't answer for a long moment. "Dom will always look out for Dom."

The car pulls up and Cav carries our bags out. An hour later, we're in the air, headed for New York. I'm antsy and need a distraction, but all I can do is worry about Holly and my aunt and Creighton, and wonder what the hell really happened to my uncle.

When Cav delivered the news, I felt a sharp stab of grief, but it wasn't the kind of pervasive grief you feel when you lose a loved one. My uncle tolerated me. My aunt was a bipolar mess of either full-on doting or complete indifference. When my uncle "went to rehab," my aunt drew inside herself. I called every week, but all she'd say was that she was fine and didn't want any visitors.

The one time I'd gone against her wishes and shown up at the house, the longtime housekeeper, Elisabetta, had greeted me with a hug, and my aunt had been sipping coffee in the sitting room. Nothing was out of the ordinary. It was all stiffly formal—her indifferent side making an appearance. After I left, I continued to call weekly, but didn't attempt to see her again. Neither of us ever mentioned my uncle, and she didn't appear concerned in the least about his whereabouts.

I wish Banner had told Cav more. Where was my uncle's body found? How did he die? I needed details and answers.

"Babe, calm down. There's nothing you can do right now. Your brother isn't helpless, and he's going to be okay."

Cav's right about that. Creighton is the least helpless person I know, but right now he must be irate. Our uncle's death is his last gasp at screwing with my brother and his companies. He probably would have loved knowing that, the cold bastard.

"I know, but Holly. The baby. Why were they even in New York? I thought they were staying in Nashville until the baby was born. It doesn't make sense."

"We'll find out everything when we get there. In the meantime, just try to chill. Worrying isn't going to do you any good either."

Objectively, I know he's right, but it's a waste of breath. Being largely cut off from communication since the day we landed in Belize has actually been strangely amazing, but now I hate not having my phone.

"How did Banner have your number anyway?"

"She must have figured out how to recover the text messages I sent myself and deleted. I'm surprised she didn't call before now, if you want the truth."

His phone rings again, as though on command. Cav looks at the display and sits up straighter. "Fuck. This isn't going to be good."

"Who is it?" I ask, but he's already answering.

"Tell me what the fuck is going on."

I can't hear the other side of the conversation, but the expression on Cav's face darkens with every word. Not good news.

"Fuck. What a disaster. They actually took him in for questioning? Like this is going to stick?"

Dom? I'm practically vibrating on my chair with the need to demand to know the whole story, but somehow I find a measure of patience and wait.

"Okay, I'll be there in a few hours. I'm not coming for him, though, I'm coming for Greer and the Karas family. Dom can get out of his own mess. He's never needed me before, and I'm sure he doesn't need me now."

My heart aches at Cav's statement. I always wished I knew my dad, and Creighton has told me so many times what an amazing guy he was. Cav clearly didn't have the same type of experience with his father, and that makes me incredibly sad for him.

He hangs up and tosses his phone to the seat.

"What happened?"

"They got a tip that your uncle had some link to Dom, and they brought him in for questioning. Basically they'll use any reason, but I'm not worried about him. Like I said, his connections are scary and there's no way they'll nail him with this."

"So you think he did it too?"

Cav frowns and shakes his head. "Hell no. Dom never gets his hands dirty and hasn't in probably thirty years. He gives orders and the soldiers carry them out. That's how it works."

This is news to me, since the inner workings of the mob aren't exactly common knowledge in my bubble. Which brings up my next question.

"Were you a soldier?"

Cav's expression shutters. "Does it matter? That's my past."

I shrug, but my curiosity level is climbing now that he's dodged the question.

"So you were." I take a stab at the truth.

His gaze, greenish-gold today, meets mine. "I never had a real designation other than Dom's errand boy."

It's not a real answer, but I'm hesitant to push further. *If it's important, he'll tell me. I'm not going to make wild conjectures in my head. We've come too far for that nonsense. I trust him.*

"So, what else did they say?"

"Not much. Your uncle was found in a hotel in Midtown. Cause of death is still unknown. A heart attack is the speculation, or possibly something that mimicked a heart attack if it was truly foul play. The questioning is standard procedure. It isn't a murder investigation . . . yet."

It's the *yet* that has me wrap my arms around myself. *Please, God, don't let it come to that.*

We each spend the rest of the flight lost in our own thoughts.

CHAPTER
THIRTY

Greer

We head to my apartment as soon as we land.

"Cannon had my phone last, the prick. I know he wouldn't keep it, though."

I search all of the likely places he might leave it—desk, nightstand, top of my dresser—but I come up empty. When I return to the kitchen, Cav is standing by the bar and holds up a padded envelope. Its label—Greer Karas, Hand Delivery. Do Not Mix With Alcohol—gives me a clue as to the contents.

"I think this is what you're looking for."

I can't keep a scowl from my face as I grab the package and tear it open. "At least he had the manners to turn it off and save the battery."

When the phone powers up, my notifications are out of control. I ignore them and make a call to Holly instead.

"Are you at the penthouse? Are you okay? Have you heard anything? What's going on?"

Cav lifts the phone from my hand and press the button for speaker. I guess it makes sense, because there's no point in me repeating the conversation to him. Holly's Southern drawl comes through loud and clear.

"That piece-of-shit bastard just had to screw with Crey one last time. I'm sorry, Greer, I know he was your uncle, but he was a prick."

"You're not telling me anything I don't already know."

"So the cops came by this morning and asked Crey to come down to the station and talk to them. They didn't arrest him. Didn't talk about bringing charges. They don't even know how the bastard died yet. Hookers and blow, is my guess. Anyway, he got done with the interview and drove out to Westchester to find your aunt, and she's MIA. So he's been looking for her for two hours. Cannon's trying to track her down too."

That's Creighton, always trying to take care of everyone and everything.

"When will they know the cause of death?"

"The autopsy should be happening now, or maybe tomorrow if they don't push it through. Obviously, a lot of people are wondering how he died."

"How are you? Are you okay?"

"My ankles are swollen, I look like I swallowed a beach ball, and this kid keeps bouncing on my bladder. Just another day in the paradise of being knocked up with the next generation of the Karas dynasty."

I can't help but laugh at her sarcastic response. "Do

you need anything?"

"I need Crey to get back here with dinner because I'm starving and the cupboards are practically bare in this place. He promised me pizza for dinner after this terrible chicken-and-rice nonsense we had delivered for lunch."

It's the perfect intro for my other question. "What are you doing back in New York anyway? I thought you were staying in Nashville until the baby was born."

"Yeah, well, that's my fault. I decided I wanted this baby to be born a New Yorker."

I wasn't going to ask why that was, but considering the excellent care facilities in the city, it couldn't be a bad decision.

"Want me to bring you over some food? I can be there in thirty minutes with whatever you want."

"That's sweet, but I'll take a rain check. Crey should be here soon. If he isn't, I'll call you back."

"Okay. Take care, Holly. The offer's on the table."

"'Bye, girl."

I hang up and look at Cav.

"What are the chances it was hookers and blow?" The question seems contrary to my optimistic tone, and against all odds, Cav smiles.

"We can always hope."

"Do you need to go find out more from your . . . people?" My question sounds hesitant, even to my ears.

"I should. I'll be back. Call me if you hear anything, and I'll do the same."

"You've got a deal."

Cav pulls me in for a quick kiss before he heads for

the door.

Two hours later I've sorted through the texts and e-mails, and then I start on my voice mails. The first one leaves a rock sitting in the pit of my stomach as I listen to a key piece of Jade's message again.

"You got a letter from the court, and one of the partners opened it. You missed the filing deadline for your prisoners' rights case, and they've been looking everywhere for the file. That prick Kevin Sunderberg told them he thought you took it with you."

"Shit. Are you kidding me?" I yell at the phone.

It's the case I took to give myself something to do, to redeem myself in some small way for being a fuckup, and I managed to screw that up too. There are two more voice mails from the firm, one from a paralegal asking about the file, and another from a partner requesting I call him immediately.

Shit. In my head, the deadline was next week. But let's be honest—I've barely thought about it. *How could I be so irresponsible?*

I remember Cannon telling me he stuffed a file in my duffel to give me something to do in Kentucky, but obviously that didn't work out the way anyone planned. Dropping to my knees beside the bag, I take everything out and find the file at the bottom. My heart in my throat, I flip it open and scan the pleadings. Sure enough, the filing deadline was last week. *I suck.*

Jesus. What do I do now? It's not like I can get fired again, but I can petition the court to waive the late filing, right? I'm a corporate lawyer, so it's not like I know how this stuff works. My do-gooder case was supposed to be easy, but apparently not.

I call the reception desk at Sterling & Michaels and get Jade. "Hey, it's Greer. I just got your voice mail."

"Girl, you are so fucked. What were you thinking taking that case file if you weren't going to do the work?"

I open my mouth to explain the absolute insanity my life has become, and close it again. No one would believe these last couple of weeks.

"It wasn't intentional. I mean, I took the file intentionally, but I didn't mean to miss the deadline. I've been out of touch with everyone for over a week."

"So I've heard. You sure know how to keep the office buzzing. You're in the freaking papers more than Miley Cyrus lately."

"I know. Trust me; it's been crazy."

"Crazy? Dating a movie star with a giant cock? Honey, I'd say your life is fucking amazing."

"It hasn't been all orgasms and rainbows, Jade. I promise. Now, tell me what I need to do with this case."

"Well, I'm not a lawyer," she starts, and I know damn well that Jade is almost done with her paralegal degree, so she probably knows more about litigation than I do at this point. "But wouldn't you be best off getting your client to fire you so you can make a motion to withdraw? I mean, you blew the filing deadline, so it's not likely he's going to want to keep you on it anyway."

"Shit, if I send him a letter, I may never hear from him, and certainly not for weeks. Looks like I'm going to Rikers again."

"Be careful, girl, that guy is a creep. I googled him after this all came out, and he's not a good guy. I mean *bad*."

"Well, he's in prison for murder, so that's not all that surprising."

"Just watch yourself. If he agrees to fire you, call the partner and tell him, and he'll get a paralegal to draft a motion for withdrawal and you're done. Bring the case file back, and you never have to deal with it again."

"Thanks, Jade. You should be a lawyer, not me."

"That's what I've been saying all along. Talk soon. I gotta grab another line."

She hangs up, and I lay my phone on the carpet beside the case file.

I'm still sitting on the floor contemplating what a gigantic screwup I am when Cav returns.

I spin around to face him. "Did you find out anything?"

"Autopsy isn't going to be done until tomorrow. Dom's already back home. There's nothing to pin on anyone until there's a cause of death. Right now, the cops are getting overexcited." He frowns down at me. "What are you doing on the floor?"

I glance down, taking in all the clothes from my bag in messy piles around me, and the case file in front of me. "I . . . um . . . forgot I had to work on this case."

Part of me wants to spill the whole situation, that I screwed up, but another part of me doesn't want Cav to know that I'm so irresponsible. This is one of those things I feel like he could live without knowing.

Cav crosses the room and offers his hand. "Must have been pretty important if you had to tear your bag apart to get at it."

I shrug, crouching down to pick it up. "I forgot about the deadline." *There, that's part of the truth.*

I walk over to the counter and set the folder down before returning to clean up the rest of the clothes. They all need to go in the laundry anyway. When I make my way back to the kitchen, Cav has the case file open, and a muscle ticks in his jaw.

"This is the guy you went to see at Rikers?"

I'm shocked he remembers, but then again, Cav seems to store away almost every detail I tell him.

"Yeah."

He slaps the file shut. "Why the hell are you still on this case if you quit your job? It makes no sense. Give it back to the firm and have them deal with it. This isn't the kind of scum you need to be dealing with. You're better than that." He turns to face me, his jaw tense, anger emblazoned on every feature.

I'm not sure how to respond to him, but the one thing I'm definitely *not* going to tell him is about my upcoming trip to Rikers. So I give him the most truth I can.

"I won't be working on it much longer. I'm turning it back over to the firm."

"Good." He scrubs his hand through his hair, the dark locks now deliciously messy. "I'm gonna take a shower, and then let's get something to eat. Check with Holly about your brother and if she hasn't heard from him, let's take dinner over to her. Pregnant woman has to eat."

I'm touched by his concern for Holly. *Cav's a good man.* "Sounds perfect. I've got a couple more calls to make, but I'll be done by the time you get out."

Cav reaches out and pulls me into him for a hug and presses a kiss to my hair. "I love you, Greer."

It's still so new to be saying the words on a regular basis, but they come so easily. "I love you too."

He releases me and heads for my bedroom. I kind of like how at home he feels in my space.

I wait until I hear the water come on in the bathroom before I call Rikers and put in a request to see my client. It's right at the end of the shift, and whoever is on the other line clearly just wants to get home.

"That's fine. I'm not checking with the prisoner today, though. Be here tomorrow by nine o'clock with the rest of the visitors, and if he refuses to see you, it'll be a wasted trip. Up to you."

"That's fine. I'll be there."

Guilt for doing this behind Cav's back gnaws at me, but this is my professional reputation I'm trying to salvage. And after tomorrow, it'll all be over anyway, and we'll go back to having no secrets between us.

CHAPTER
THIRTY-ONE

Greer

Have you ever had a premonition? Or even just an uneasy feeling that something is going to go horribly wrong? I can't shake the feeling on the cab ride out to Rikers.

Yes, cab ride. I could have called Ed, but then this trip would have been run through Creighton, and I definitely didn't want my brother to know about it any more than I wanted Cav to be aware.

I can't shake that feeling, though, like something terrible is going to happen. With my luck lately, there'll be a prison riot with a full lockdown, and I'll get stuck inside. Cav and Creighton will have to tear Rikers apart brick by brick to get me out. I can only imagine the lecture I'd get from Creighton then.

Maybe I should have brought Ed . . .

Last night after I called the prison, I called Holly to see if she wanted some dinner, company, or both. Creighton had just walked in the door with her favorite fried chicken in the city, and she was happily moaning about how amazing it was. Creighton liberated the phone from her.

"You're home?"

"Yes, I came as soon as I heard. Is there anything I can do?"

Creighton sighed before replying, and once again I felt like the little sister who was a constant screwup. *I'm not that girl anymore.*

"Nothing you can do. We're all just waiting on the autopsy results, and that'll determine what's next."

"And Dom?" My question was quiet because I didn't want Cav to overhear.

"He's in charge of looking out for himself. He doesn't need either of us worrying about him."

That was probably the truth.

"And Aunt Katherine?"

"Elisabetta said the last she knew, she was heading to an overnight spa place and hadn't come back yet. She didn't remember which one. I've got Cannon trying to track her down."

So once again, my brother had everything under control, down to checking with the housekeeper. "Okay. Well, let me know if you need anything from me."

"Just stay out of trouble, Greer."

Again, the fuckup feeling grew exponentially.

"Will do. Glad you're okay, Creighton."

Recalling the conversation while in the back of a cab headed for Rikers Island almost surely makes it a little more ironic.

"Just stay out of trouble, Greer."

That's what I'm working on, brother dearest.

I'll be in and out, and no one will be the wiser. All I need is my client's signature on the letter requesting my withdrawal from the case, and this will all become a bad memory.

The process to get into the prison is almost as hard as getting out. Because I don't have a formal appointment, I have to wait longer than I hoped, and the Saturday crowd waiting to visit loved ones is out of control.

One woman waits with a baby bouncing on her lap. She's dressed neatly in black pants and a pink-and-white striped shirt that matches the baby's onesie.

Is she visiting the father? I can't even imagine what it would be like to have to stare at the man you loved through inches of bulletproof glass or across a table while he's wearing a prison jump suit.

I glance down at the clock on my phone for the seventy-seventh time. I told Cav this morning that I was going to meet someone from work because there were still some loose ends to tie up on my exit from the firm and handing over the case. I don't know if he didn't realize today was Saturday, but he didn't ask any other questions.

It isn't a lie, I tell myself as the guilt creeps up again. *But it definitely isn't the whole truth either.*

Cav's preoccupation could probably be chalked up to the fact that he was heading to meet Dom, which sounded more than a little ominous to me.

Finally, an hour later, I'm called in to meet with Stephen Cardelli. A rush of relief sweeps through me because for the last thirty minutes, I truly thought he was going to decline to meet, which would screw me on multiple levels. But he didn't.

As I walk into the interview room, I'm mentally rehearsing the very apologetic and persuasive conversation I'm about to have with Mr. Cardelli. I'm seated in the molded plastic chair bolted to the floor and table when the guard brings him in.

His gray hair is greasy and falling over his forehead in chunks, and his skin is flushed red, either from exertion or something else. His faded blue gaze fixes on me and intensifies.

I've never truly understood the real meaning of feeling my skin crawl until now. But under the scrutiny of Cardelli, I absolutely do. Both Jade and Cav's warnings run through my head, highlighted in bright colors and underlined several times.

"You've got fifteen minutes," the guard says, locking Cardelli's shackles into the bolts on the floor and table.

This is new—and disturbing. Did something happen since last time to necessitate the extra security precautions?

The man in front of me gives me a cruel, disgusting

smile, and I know I'm not going to pose the question to him.

He hasn't even opened his mouth yet and I already know I've made a horrible mistake. I shouldn't have come here. I should have let the firm deal with it.

My belly flips with the premonition from earlier.

"You got some good timing in some ways and shit timing in others," Cardelli says.

I launch into my rehearsed spiel right then. "I'm sorry, Mr. Cardelli; I owe you an apology. I missed the filing deadline on your case, and I'm not certain whether or not the court is going to waive it. They should because it was my mistake and not yours, but either way, it happened and the firm is going to try to fix it. Everyone agrees that the best alternative is to have another lawyer take over your case."

His expression grows thunderous. "You fucked my shit up? What the hell? You're the fanciest lawyers in town. That ain't right."

Sitting in front of this disgusting man, I actually feel guilt. He's the one trapped behind bars, and I have the professional obligation to discharge my duties according to the rules of the court, and I couldn't even do that. Now my solution to him is *please let me off the case and maybe someone can fix it.* This is his life, and all I care about is getting myself out of this situation. *Nice, Greer.*

"I'm very sorry. It was an oversight, and it won't happen again once your case is transferred. I'm not actually at the firm anymore, so you can see it makes sense that I shouldn't continue to handle your case. All you need to do is sign this letter, and I'll get the ball rolling to have another attorney assigned to you." I pull the letter from the file on the table and a golf pencil.

Shit. Should I even give him the pencil? They're permissible, but couldn't he still stab someone with it?

Rather than reaching for the pencil, he leans back in his seat and rests his hands near his lap, as close as the shackles will let him get.

"No."

What? He can't say no. I mean, he obviously *can*, but that's not how this is supposed to go.

"Mr. Cardelli, I don't think you're considering this fully. Another much more senior attorney from the firm will be assigned to your case," I say, crossing my fingers below the table because I honestly have no idea who will be working on the case. But if I know the firm, they should do damage control and not give it to a junior associate again. "This is a good thing. Actually, a great thing for you."

His chapped lips form a smirk that stirs up an icky feeling in my stomach. "You want off this case bad and you can't get off without my say-so." His words are mocking, almost triumphant.

"The court may remove me anyway." I cross my arms when I deliver the bluff.

"I don't know about that. But what I do know is that in here," he jerks his head behind him toward the door, "and on the outside, you don't get something for nothing." He leans forward again, resting both forearms on the table. "So you're gonna do something for me, and then we'll see about getting you uninvolved."

I didn't come here prepared to bargain with the guy. Actually, I didn't expect him to put up any kind of resistance when offered a more senior and experienced lawyer. *What can he possibly want from me?*

"What are you talking about?" I keep my tone firm and cool. I will not let him know that this has me rattled.

"The Innocence Project. You're going to lay out my case and send it to them so I can get out of here."

Shit. That's what he wants. I stare at the man in shackles with dead eyes and a cruel mouth, knowing that there's no way I can, in good conscience, help him get free.

But the Innocence Project could take years to deal with his case. They're absolutely inundated with requests, and besides, whatever this guy was locked up for, he probably *did* do it, so there would be no grounds for releasing him.

"You give me an outline of the facts of your case and why you think you've been wrongfully convicted, and I'll put it together in a way that's logical and organized for you to submit. Right now, right here, and you sign this letter before I leave the room."

I glance at the clock on the wall. We still have twelve minutes. *How is it possible only three minutes have passed?*

"Then you better hurry and start writing, girl, because this is going to take the whole time. If we're not done when time's up, I'm not signing anything until you come back to finish the job. Then I'll sign your shit so you can get off the case and go get your nails done, or whatever fancy broads like you spend your time doing." He practically spits out those last words.

I pull out a legal pad and retrieve the pencil from the table. "All right. You've got a deal. Let's go."

He looks around the room, as if checking to see who might overhear. The guard is standing eight feet away, his thumbs tucked into the belt of his uniform.

Finally, Cardelli starts. "Last time you were here, I probably woulda gotten shanked for even opening my mouth about this shit and naming names, but now that the gossip mill says that rat bastard Casso is going down for murder, shit is changing."

Everything in me stills when he says the name *Casso*.

CHAPTER
THIRTY-TWO

Cav

Once again I find myself standing before my father's desk, but this time, I'm not here because of something I've done. I'm here to find out if my help is needed to get this fucking mess under control.

"You think they have the balls to bring charges?"

Dom, still looking every inch the indifferent king in his tall-backed leather chair, raises and lowers his shoulders in a shrug. "Not if they know what's good for them."

"Would the charges stick if they brought them?" The question is one I wouldn't have dared to ask years ago.

"Fuck no. Not only because I didn't kill the bastard, but because nothing ever sticks when they bring it. I've been clean for years. There's nothing tying me to any of that shit."

This I believe because, like I told Greer, Dom Casso

doesn't get his hands dirty. I never figured he killed her uncle, but I assume he knows who did.

"You sure they can't tie you back to it?" Once again, I'm pushing the boundaries of what's smart. Dom does not like to be questioned by anyone. And doubted? That's grounds for a verbal flaying.

"You think I'm an idiot, boy?"

His tone and words take me back to being fifteen again for a second, but I'm not that kid. I'm a grown man and here to see if he needs help.

"I think you're a lot of things, Dom. And if you don't need my help, I'll be on my way." I turn and head for the door where his two bodyguards are standing.

"I'm not done talking to you."

I pause and turn. "What?" My tone carries my impatience across the room.

Dom doesn't miss it, and his voice is ripe with displeasure. "The Karas girl. You didn't follow my orders. What the fuck do you think you're doing? She's not for you."

I've heard this all before, and hell, I've told myself the same thing.

"Whether she's for me or not, she's mine and I won't give her up."

He crosses his arms over his chest, and his lip curls. "And what do you think's gonna happen if she ever finds out the real reason I kicked your ass out of this town and you ended up on a Greyhound to Hollywood?"

CHAPTER
THIRTY-THREE

Greer

My hands are nerveless, paralyzed into useless claws, and I've forgotten how to write. The pencil tumbles from my fingers as he speaks. But Cardelli is so caught up in his own story, he doesn't notice the physical toll his words are taking on me. Ice crystals form in my lungs, and my fight for breath turns desperate. As I suck in small but precious gulps of oxygen, he keeps speaking, oblivious to the panic attack crashing into me across the table.

Get it together, Greer. Before he notices.

Curling my hands into fists, I stab my nails into my palms, and the sharp pain helps me derail the downward spiral. But not completely.

Death.

Murder.

Unclenching my fists, I stretch my hands out, watching them shake for a moment before grabbing the white barrel of the pencil. It slides from my grip twice before I'm able to scrawl letters on the legal pad in front of me as Stephen Cardelli continues with the story of how Cavanaugh Casso framed him for a murder Cav committed.

Cav is a murderer.

The words hammer with unrelenting pressure into my temples as I struggle to keep breathing.

In.

Out.

In.

Out.

"Donnigan carried out the hit, and when Casso's bastard kid Cavanaugh found out, he took out Donnigan and they pinned it on me 'cause I pissed Casso off by slapping around one of the girls at his club. I've been rotting in here for three fucking years, keeping my mouth shut so I didn't get shanked and end up bleeding out in the showers. But now that word on the block is that Casso's going down, I'm done keeping quiet. I want out, and I know Casso paid off the cops who took me in and planted the piece they used to kill Donnigan in my shit. So tell that to your fuckin' Innocence Project and get me the hell out of here."

My vision blurs when I look down at the notepad before me. I can't read a single thing I've written. *Tears*, I realize. They're gathering in my eyes but haven't fallen. I blink them back. *I will not cry in front of this man.*

When the guard strides over to the table, interrupting Cardelli's monologue, I'm limp with relief. *I don't want to hear any more.*

"Time's up."

"I ain't done."

"Too fucking bad."

I could protest. This is an attorney-client meeting, but I barely have it together enough to stand, let alone put together a coherent argument for the guard. Not when all I want is to get as far away from this place as fast as humanly possible to tear apart Cardelli's story in my head.

It can't be true. Can it?

Following the guard, I return to the waiting area on shaky legs. Everything I thought I knew has been shredded into tiny, unrecognizable pieces.

It can't be true, my head argues again. *Right?*

But Cardelli's devastating accusations dog my steps, threatening to steal the future I was starting to believe I could have.

Cav killed someone. In cold blood. Execution style. In an alley.

CHAPTER
THIRTY-FOUR

Cav

Dom's question follows me all the way home, but Greer isn't there. Part of me wishes she was so I could tell her everything right now. Get it over with. Come clean. No more secrets.

A bigger part of me is grateful for the empty apartment because I need time to figure out how.

I stare at the floor where she sat with that file.

Of all the fucking cases in the world, how did she end up with that one?

I could have asked Dom to take care of the problem, but the words wouldn't come.

I'm not going to lose her.

I just hope to hell I'm right.

CHAPTER
THIRTY-FIVE

Greer

I tell the cabbie to take me to Banner's. I can't go home. I need to tell someone what I just learned so they can tell me what the hell I'm supposed to do. I'm lost. Utterly and completely.

Can my judgment really be that bad?

I pay my outrageous cab fare and wave weakly to Banner's doorman.

"Ms. Karas. How are you?"

"Fine, thanks." The rote greeting comes out automatically, and I hope he can't tell that I'm anything but fine. He nods to me, and I head to the elevator.

My mind is going in a million directions when the door opens onto her floor and I stumble out. Banner's welcome mat reads GO THE FUCK AWAY, but I don't take it personally. It doesn't apply to me. Never has.

I knock on the door, although *pound* might be more accurate. There's no answer. No footsteps. Nothing.

It's Saturday. *She's gotta be here. I need her to be here.*

I pull out my phone and make the call. "Come on . . . come on . . ."

From inside the apartment, I hear the unmistakable sounds of the *Golden Girls* theme song that Banner picked as my ringtone.

Thank God she's home.

"What's goin' on, G?" Banner's voice sounds huskier than normal.

"Sorry. Did I wake you?"

"Umm. Yeah. No biggie. What's going on?"

"I'm outside your door."

"Oh. Shit. Okay. Hold on." And then she hangs up.

The dead bolts slide back moments later and Banner opens the door partway. She's dressed in a man's white T-shirt and nothing else.

"Oh. Shit." I echo her words. "Am I interrupting?"

Banner shakes her head but doesn't open the door further. "No. Of course not. You're never an interruption. What's up?"

The deep rumble of a voice coming from behind her means that if my best friend were wearing pants, they'd be *liar, liar, pants on fire.*

The voice grows louder and the drawl strikes me as familiar. Banner's face pales in color, but she's pretending he's not inside.

That can't be Logan Brantley. It's not possible.

Except it is him.

Banner closes the door a fraction of an inch, but it's too late. She adopts a casual mien, leaning against the doorjamb like there's not a shirtless giant of a man standing in her living room, just within my range of vision.

"What's happening? You're awfully dressed up for an unemployed Saturday morning. When did you get back? Did they give a cause of death? What's happening?" Banner's questions come at me rapid-fire, but that's not the unusual part. It's the bouncing of her leg.

I don't know what's going on here, but whatever it is, my friend doesn't want me to know yet. And right now, I can live with that.

"Uh, yesterday. Not yet on the autopsy. I . . . just wanted to see if you were up for grabbing lunch. But we can do it tomorrow or whenever."

Banner nods enthusiastically. "Tomorrow's good. I want all the details. Call me?"

She's already pushing the door shut when I agree and turn for the elevator.

Maybe I'm dreaming. Maybe today isn't real. How can any of this be real?

Banner's doorman waves down a cab, and I climb in. Creighton's address comes out of my mouth instinctively. When in doubt, I run to my big brother.

Holly opens the door and draws me in for a hug over her huge belly.

"How you doin', girl? You okay?"

I shake my head when Holly pulls back. "No. I—I'm not. Is Crey here?"

"No, he's at the office taking care of a few things. I expect him back in a few hours."

Hours. I don't want to wait minutes to tell someone what's bottled up in my head. I question the wisdom of laying this on a pregnant woman, but Holly's one of the most grounded people I know.

"Can I tell you something?"

"Of course. Anything. But if you need to hide a body, we're gonna have to call your brother. I'm not allowed to lift anything heavy."

Choking out a laugh, I follow as she leads me into the living area and pulls me down onto the couch beside her. As soon as we're seated, she pauses. "Should I have grabbed the moonshine? Because you look awfully serious, Greer."

I can't contain it any longer. I blurt out the words. "Cav might have killed someone."

Both of Holly's dark eyebrows shoot toward her hairline. "Come again?"

"I think Cav killed someone. And framed someone else for the murder."

To her credit, Holly doesn't freak out. "You're gonna have to start from the beginning."

The story pours out of me. The prisoners' rights case. Rikers. Dom Casso being taken in for questioning. And then what Stephen Cardelli told me. With every word, I fight to hold back the impending tears.

Holly must hear it in my voice because she reaches for

a box of tissues on the side table and sets them between us. "Well, hell, that's a lot to take in on decaf coffee."

"I don't . . . I don't know what to believe." I feel like I'm fighting for every breath.

Holly lays a hand on my knee. "It's going to be okay, Greer. If I learned anything over the last year, it's not to jump to conclusions. If you're thinking of running, don't. You need to know the truth first."

A vision of that iconic scene in *A Few Good Men* runs through my head. The one where Jack Nicholson is yelling about Tom Cruise not being able to handle the truth.

Can I handle the truth? I squeeze my eyes shut and bite the inside of my cheek. I don't want to put the possibility out into the universe, but the words come anyway.

"What if Cardelli is telling the truth?"

Holly nods, as if lining up what she's going to say in her own head. "So what if he is? Can you live with it?"

My stomach revolts, twisting into knots and flipping in a double back handspring. Good to know one part of my body is capable of that.

Could I live with that?

"I don't know. I mean . . . could you?" My voice sounds hoarse and shredded, like I gargled a mouthful of broken glass on the way up here.

"I'd be surprised if your brother hasn't killed someone. Maybe even be a little disappointed," Holly deadpans.

"Oh my God." A wave of giggles escapes me. It's like someone cued the comic relief.

Holly waits until I'm holding my gut and using the tissues to wipe away the tears of laughter.

"Seriously, though, you have to be able to answer that question for yourself. If by some chance what that guy said is true, you need to walk into that conversation with Cav knowing what you can and can't live with. You love him."

The last part is a statement rather than a question, but I reply anyway.

"Yes."

"Do you think he's capable of something like this?"

That one I don't have an answer to. "I don't know."

"In your heart of hearts, you have to have a sense of him."

I lace my fingers together and squeeze. "He's a good man. I don't care what Creighton says about him. I know that to my soul."

"Then go with your gut on this. Do you think you'd fall in love with a cold-blooded killer?"

The weight of her question presses me back into the cushions of the leather sectional. Trusting my gut has had varying amounts of success. Okay, that's a lie, mostly crap results. But with Cav, I don't have anything else I can trust . . . except my heart.

"I couldn't. Could I?"

Holly doesn't answer me. At least, not right away. "I guess he's the only one who can answer that question for you."

I reach out and clamp a hand over her knee. A little too hard, so we both jump.

"Jesus, Greer. What the heck?"

"Sorry, but I need you to promise that you're not going to tell Creighton any of this. Not that I was here. Not about Cav. Or Cardelli. Nothing. I don't want to come between you, but you can't say anything. Swear to me that you won't. Because if this is all a load of jailhouse bullshit, Creighton can't ever know I considered it seriously. I need a sister-in-law oath in blood."

Holly draws in a breath and releases it. "If it's true, he's going to find out. He *always* finds out."

"I know." I meet her gaze, more serious than I've ever seen it. "But it can't be true. So he's never going to find out, right?"

I get a nod from her. "But I'm not cuttin' myself and smearing our bloody hands together. It's not safe for the baby."

We both stand, and I wrap my arms around her neck. "Thank you for listening."

"What are sisters for?"

CHAPTER

THIRTY-SIX

Cav

"Hey, I wondered what happened to you. Hungry? Or did you grab something while you were out?"

I'm holding the mustard bottle in midair when Greer walks through the door, a big black purse clutched to her side. She looks up at my words, but it's like she doesn't recognize me or comprehend my question. It's the long blank stare that clues me in to the fact that something is off.

"Greer? You okay?"

She shakes her head, as if snapping out of the trance she seems to be in. "Sorry, what'd you say?"

I set the mustard bottle down on the counter and come around the island. Greer clutches the purse tighter to her side as I get closer. A file folder sticks out the top. The one from yesterday.

I swallow, knowing it's time. "You get your work stuff

sorted out?"

Greer bites her bottom lip so hard, it goes white. She waits too long before releasing it and answering. "I don't know."

A feeling of dread pools in my stomach.

"Why did you tell me he was dangerous?" Her voice sounds pained, as if the words are torn from her throat. "How did you even know who he was?"

It's now or never. "I need to tell you something."

Greer squeezes her eyes shut like she can't bear to look at me. "I've heard a lot of things today already."

The dread multiplies. *She can't know.*

"Where were you, Greer?" The words come out rough.

Her eyelids blink open, and the dark brown eyes of the girl I've fallen in love with over and over are shiny with unshed tears. "Rikers. Trying to get Stephen Cardelli to sign a letter stating he no longer wanted me as his lawyer so I could withdraw from the case."

"What did he tell you?" I've never wanted an answer to a question less.

"Something that I don't think could possibly be true." A tear spills onto her cheek. "Tell me it's not true, Cav." Her face twists into the look I've feared. The one I knew would cut me off at the knees. Confusion, revulsion, brokenhearted pain. They're all there.

"It's not what you're thinking, Greer. I swear to you, it's not what you're thinking." *No,* I add to myself, *because it's worse.*

"Did you kill a man named Donnigan and frame Cardelli for the murder?" Her voice shakes as she asks the question point-blank.

I can't lie to her, even though the words tear into me like the rounds I unloaded in that alley.

"Yes."

Greer sucks in a short breath and her hand goes to her mouth. Her eyes squeeze shut, and each tear that falls is another jab through my heart.

What kind of man makes his girl cry?

I have to make her understand. "I did it to protect you."

Her eyes snap open, confusion clear on her face.

"What?" It comes out as a whisper.

"He didn't tell you everything. He couldn't tell you everything because he doesn't know everything. You got one part of the story without any context, and I swear to you, whatever you're thinking right now is going to be different when you know it all."

Greer drops her purse to the floor and jams both hands into her hair. "Then tell me everything because I'm seriously losing my shit here, Cav. I don't know whether to call the police or call you a lawyer."

Another direct hit. *I can't lose her.* I have to talk fast. She needs to understand what happened.

"Do you remember the day you called me to meet you at the hospital because Tracey had been killed in a hit-and-run?"

Just saying the words brings the memory back in vivid detail . . .

I knew something was wrong the moment Greer's shattered voice came on the line.

"The hospital just called me. I'm Tracey's emergency contact on her phone. Something happened, and they need me to come down there." Her voice shook. "It's gotta be bad. They don't call you like this unless it's bad. They won't let me talk to her. Will you please come?"

She was right—it had to be bad. A pang of sympathy went through me for whatever was about to unfold.

I'd met Tracey a few weeks before, and she was a sweet girl. She and Greer had been attached at the hip before I entered the picture. I couldn't tell you how many times I'd watched the two of them together before I'd crossed the line and started talking to Greer. If I hadn't known Greer was the only girl in the Karas family, I might have mistaken them for sisters. Both had long dark hair, similar builds, and shopped at the same stores.

I grabbed my tool bag and headed for the maintenance closet. "Of course. Where are you? Where do we need to go?"

She breathed into the phone, and it sounded like a sigh of relief.

"I'm at my place. I just got done with a meeting with Creighton. I'm walking out the door now for Harlem Hospital. I don't know why they'd take her there."

"I'm at the school. I'll be out in front of your building in fifteen. Wait for me, baby girl. I'm coming with you."

When we entered the hospital twenty-five minutes later, Greer's grip on my hand threatened to break it, her growing fear palpable with every step.

I squeezed her hand back, wanting to remind her that she wasn't alone. Whatever happened, we would face it together.

The woman at the desk directed us to a private waiting room, and I already knew what was coming. Tracey was dead. They were going to tell us.

Greer hadn't realized it yet, but she clung to my side as though her body already knew.

A doctor came in, looking haggard in her white coat and blue scrubs.

"Are you Greer Karas?" she asked.

"Yes, that's me. I . . . you called about Tracey? Is she okay? What happened?" Greer asked all the questions any person in this room would ask.

The doctor's face turned sympathetic. "I'm so sorry, Ms. Karas. Ms. Mullins was in an accident . . . and she didn't make it."

Even though I knew it was coming, the words still punched me in the gut.

"No!" Greer's wail echoed in the tiny room as she threw herself into my arms, tears already falling and soaking my shirt. Maybe she knew it was coming too.

"I'm very sorry for your loss, Ms. Karas."

"What happened?" I choked out the question.

The doctor lifted her gaze from Greer to me. "There was a hit-and-run. Ms. Mullins was jogging, and according to the eyewitnesses, the car failed to stop at the light and hit her."

Greer's body shook with sobs as I wrapped my arms around her tighter. She sounded like she was being destroyed from the inside out.

"Who would do something like that?" Greer's question came out somewhere between irate and heartbroken.

"We're not sure, Ms. Karas. The driver didn't stop. The police have been notified, and there will certainly be an investigation."

Greer pulled away from me to wrap her arms around her waist and hunch forward, rocking back and forth. She didn't know how to process this kind of grief. I laid an arm across her shoulders and tugged her against my side again, hoping the contact would give her strength.

"Would you like to say good-bye?" the doctor asked.

My heart cracked at the tears streaking Greer's face when she raised her head.

"Good-bye?"

"Yes, Ms. Karas. We're going to move Ms. Mullins shortly, so if you'd like . . ."

I held my breath, waiting for Greer to respond. Would she want to see her friend?

"Yes. Of course. Where do I go?"

"You can come right this way, ma'am." The doctor gestured for the door. "And, sir, you're welcome to come along . . . for support."

Greer stood on shaky legs, and I kept my arm wrapped around her waist. "Yes, he's coming."

We followed the doctor down the white hallway through double steel doors and past a half dozen treatment-type bays, some with open curtains, some with closed.

The doctor paused outside one toward the end. "She's

at peace. She's not suffering. She has some bruising around her face, but most of her injuries were internal."

I wondered if she went quickly, but I wasn't going to ask any questions right now.

Greer nodded at the doctor and reached down to grab my hand. "Okay."

We walked inside the small room, and Greer shrank back from the form on the bed. "Oh my God." Her words shook as the sobs broke through.

She buried her face in my shirt again like she couldn't bear to see what was in front of her. I didn't blame her. Tracey looked like she was sleeping, but the bruising around her cheek and temple were dark and ugly. Her blue sweatshirt had been cut down the center, no doubt so they could work on her, but was folded so it covered her chest completely. A sheet was pulled up to her waist.

Greer stepped away from me again, and what came out of her mouth shocked me even more.

"It should have been me." The words were quiet, carrying all the sorrow and regret in the world. "We were supposed to run together. That stupid couch to half marathon. But I had to bail today because Creighton needed me to come to a meeting and sign a bunch of papers."

She reached out and touched the ends of Tracey's dark hair before yanking her hand back.

"She's even wearing my sweatshirt." Greer dropped to her knees beside the bed, pressing her forehead into Tracey's hand. "I'm so sorry, Trace. I'm so sorry."

Her body shuddered with the force of her sobs, and I knelt beside her to lend her my strength.

Greer is staring at me in the kitchen, and I know we're both reliving the memory together. Her eyes fill with tears.

"What does that have to do with anything?"

"It wasn't an accident. Donnigan's the one who killed her." I pause, taking a deep breath before I give Greer the truth that's going to rock the very foundation of her world. "But he fucked up. You were the target. They'd taken a hit out on you."

CHAPTER

THIRTY-SEVEN

Greer

"What? No. That's— No." I'm not making sense, but neither is what Cav is telling me. I blink back the tears stinging my eyes at those horrible moments in the hospital as Cav nods slowly, letting me take in the truth.

"Yes. She was collateral damage. She was wearing your sweatshirt. She had the hood up. Donnigan thought he got you."

"Why? Who would do something . . . I don't under-stand." *A hit? On me?* I feel like I've stepped into an alter-nate universe. "How?"

"Your brother was slashing and burning his way through companies. Hostile takeovers. I'm sure you re-member."

Oh, I remember. Creighton wasn't a popular guy then or now. He'd built his empire by acquiring companies that were ripe targets, whether they wanted to be acquired or not, and then tore them apart, selling the unprofitable pieces and then installing new management teams to turn a profit. I know this because I'm the majority shareholder of many of them through my trust. The day Tracey died—*was killed*—I was signing paperwork for another new acquisition.

But none of this makes sense.

"The moment you said *it should have been me*, I knew something was off. Dom had me watching you for a reason. You took too many risks, and your brother had too many enemies. Creighton was so deep in his business, he didn't realize what kind of danger you could be in, which is why Dom stepped in. I guess he felt like it was something he owed Creighton. I went to Dom about Tracey, and he started digging. That's how I found out about Donnigan and the hit. Three days after the accident."

My mind races to recall three days after the hospital. Tracey's funeral. And the next day, Cav stood me up, leaving me waiting alone on the Top of the Rock.

The accusations leveled by Cardelli at Rikers this morning add to the puzzle pieces snapping together in my brain as Cav continues.

"According to Donnigan, an owner of a company Creighton took over had connections to one of the Irish families, and decided to take something from your brother the same way he felt his company had been stolen. And what he decided to take was you."

The layers of shock are piling on, and all I feel is numbness. It's as if I'm standing outside my body and watching the scene from a few steps away. *This isn't really my life. This isn't really happening.*

"So you killed him." The words come out remarkably calm, but instead of a question, it's a statement.

Cav answers anyway. "Yes. Because I knew he'd come back after you as soon as he realized he'd gotten the wrong girl. I wasn't gonna let that happen."

Leaning on the counter for support, I stare at him. There's no remorse in Cav's expression.

"And then you left town without a word."

"Yes."

"Because you killed someone."

"To protect you." Cav's hazel gaze drills into mine. "I would've done anything to protect you."

My knees shake, on the verge of giving out, and I yank the stool over and collapse onto it. "You killed him. To protect me. And then you left."

"I didn't go to Dom until it was done. He cursed me for being a stupid son of a bitch, even though he would've ordered it done anyway. But the trail needed to be covered. Someone had to take the fall. And for some misguided reason, he wasn't gonna let me take the rap for it."

Another stab of pain pierces my heart. "You would've gone to prison. Like Cardelli. For life."

"I know."

In my head, my lawyer's brain says Cav should be the one in prison, but the rest of me is telling it to shut the hell up. "He was going to kill me?"

Cav nods. "Absolutely. He wouldn't get paid until he'd completed the contract."

I had been a *contract. Jesus fucking Christ.* How is that even possible?

"So you framed Cardelli," I murmur, looking down at the file before me.

"He's a rapist and a murderer in his own right. He raped a waitress out back behind one of Dom's clubs three nights before. Put her in the hospital. Dom wanted him off the street, and it fell together. Prison or death—that was his choice. So he went down for the murder."

Everything Cav is saying is so unbelievably foreign to me, I don't know how to comprehend it.

Street justice. Is that what this was? Honor among thieves?

It doesn't change the fact that my boyfriend is a murderer.

"I didn't know how to tell you. I didn't . . . fuck, Greer. I didn't want you to know."

My gaze lifts to Cav as he shoves his hands into his hair.

"Were you ever going to tell me?" I don't know why the answer to that question matters so much to me, but it does. I need to know. Would he have kept this from me forever?

He closes his eyes for a moment before opening them. "You want the truth?"

My heart hammers in my chest.

"Yes."

"I never wanted to tell you. This isn't something you need to understand or know exists. You live in a bubble, Greer, and I would do everything in my power to keep it untainted. I never wanted you to feel what you're feeling right now. I wanted to protect you from everything, even myself."

Pain radiates through my chest, like it's cracking open as he continues to speak.

"But when I saw that file yesterday, it was the sign I needed to know I was making the wrong choice. I can't keep the past buried forever, no matter how much I wish I could. I knew I had to tell you the truth."

How can I believe him? My judgment has been flawed every step of the way. Bad decision after bad decision, just like I told Holly. How can I trust myself to know what to feel about this?

I slide off the stool and pick up my discarded bag from the floor. "I have to go."

"What? You're not—"

"I have to go," I repeat, more forcefully this time. "I need to think. I can't be around you right now."

Cav's jaw tightens. "You're walking away. Now that you know everything, you're walking away."

I squeeze my eyes shut because seeing the shattered expression on his face unleashes wave after wave of pain inside me.

I bump into the door and grab the handle. "What else is out there, Cav? What other huge secrets are you keeping? The hits keep coming, and I don't know how many more I can handle." My voice is shaking, and my need to flee is growing.

I have to get out of here.

"Nothing, Greer! There's nothing else. You know it all.

Except maybe this." His gaze intensifies as I brace myself for another blow. His voice is steady and firm. "I would do it again to protect you. There's *nothing* I wouldn't do to protect you. I loved you then, and I fucking love you now. If you can't love me knowing that I'd give up everything to keep you safe, including spend the rest of my life in prison, then this is over. There's nothing here to fight for."

And that's the blow. The one that catches me in the stomach and sends me stumbling out the door, tears falling from my eyes.

CHAPTER
THIRTY-EIGHT

Greer

How do you deal with the fact the man you loved killed someone to protect you? And that he'd do it again without remorse or apology?

Cav's right. I do live in a bubble, and in my bubble, this concept doesn't exist.

I slip into a cab and head back to Creighton and Holly's. I don't know where else to go.

The doorman rings the apartment, and I go up the private elevator.

Holly opens the door and the moment she sees me, her face falls from a smile to a frown.

"Oh hell. What happened?" She pulls me inside, and I follow her to where Creighton is standing near the kitchen counter as he talks on the phone.

"Make the arrangements. I'll call you back." He hangs

up, his eyes raking over me. "Where is that bastard? I'm going to kill him."

His choice of words unleashes a peal of hysterical laughter from me, and I sound like a crazy person.

I look to Holly and she shakes her head. *She didn't tell him.* But I'm going to. Because at this point, I have no idea what else to do.

I'm attempting to wipe the tears from my eyes when I reply to my brother. "How about no one dies today."

"What the hell happened?" Creighton's voice leaves no room for anything but the truth.

"Do you remember Tracey?"

Confusion creases my brother's brow, and I start from the beginning, spilling everything.

When I finish, Holly is staring at me, looking even more shocked than she did earlier today, and Creighton's expression is unreadable.

"I think I just wrote a new song in my head. Am I the most terrible sister-in-law in the world if I tell you to keep talking, but I need to write it down quick?"

It seems impossible, but I grunt out a laugh. "No, go right ahead. If you need to write the number-one single to your new album, *I Killed a Hitman to Save my Girl and then Left Her for Three Years without Telling Her What Happened,* feel free."

Holly shoots me a smile that looks a little sad, but grabs a pen off the counter and a leather notebook. Creighton is still watching me.

Another thought hits me and I freeze. "Oh my God, did you know?"

Creighton shakes his head slowly. "No. But there's something missing in this explanation."

"What?"

"How the fuck Dom knew the ins and outs of that deal, and apparently everything I've ever done. He has someone on the inside, and there's only one person who would know that much. I just never thought he'd betray me."

Everything inside me goes cold.

"Cannon?" I whisper.

"No way." This comes from Holly.

Creighton grabs his phone and calls his second-in-command. "Get to my place. Now." He hangs up without waiting for a response.

We all wait in the most painfully awkward silence of our lives. Holly keeps scribbling, and Creighton and I just stare at each other.

"What do I do? About Cav?"

Creighton's jaw tenses and his lips flatten into a thin line. He doesn't speak for several moments as he works out the answer in his head.

"I can't decide if I want to kill him or welcome him to the family," he finally says.

"What?"

"How can I fault the man for doing whatever was necessary to keep you safe? Especially when I didn't even realize there was a threat?" Creighton looks meaningfully at Holly. "I'd kill for her—without hesitation or a second thought. If he loves you half as much as I love her, then I understand his reasoning."

I freeze in shock for several beats. "Are you serious?"

Creighton meets my gaze. "As serious as murder. Now you have to decide whether you can live with it. Life isn't black and white, Greer. He protected you, and a dangerous man went to prison. What you do from here is up to you."

This isn't the response I expected from my brother. I thought he'd be chairing the *railroad Cav out of town and preferably to prison* committee.

A long sigh escapes my lips, and I press into both pounding temples with three fingers each. "I can't believe you'd leave a decision like this in my hands. All I've done is fuck up one thing after another."

My brother's expression turns even more serious. "If you think I've made all the right decisions, then I'm afraid you've got me on the wrong pedestal. You're a smart woman, Greer. All this shit with Cav just tells me one thing— you've got no common sense when it comes to him because you're so damn in love with him. How can I judge you for that? Whatever decision you make needs to be the right one for you. We'll support you, no matter what."

A knock on the door sounds before I can respond.

Cannon.

Creighton lets him in, and Holly and I glance at each other nervously. My brother doesn't wait long enough for Cannon to step into the living room before he fires his question off.

"How long have you been feeding information to Dominic Casso about me, my family, and my businesses?"

Cannon's eyes widen for only a fraction of a second before he recovers his composure. I expect a denial, but when he opens his mouth, it's the truth that comes out.

"Since a year after you hired me."

Oh my God.

Creighton's fists clench; otherwise there's no sign of emotion from him. "Why?"

"Because you're my family, and I'd do anything to protect you, even make a deal with the devil."

His words sound so much like Cav's, I'm taken aback. *I'd do anything to protect you.*

"Are you still giving him information?" Creighton's tone would make an infantry quake with fear.

"Yes."

My brother's jaw muscle ticks while he absorbs the answer. "You're fired."

Cannon's face drains of color. "Crey—"

"I can't have a leak in my own house. Not from you. Not to him."

Cannon's nostrils flare as he crosses his arms. "I'm not going to apologize. I did the right thing. He has connections you can't imagine. We never would've gotten this far without—"

The words of doom. No one should ever intimate that my brother didn't get to where he is on his own. I think Creighton believes he could part the Red Sea à la Moses through sheer force of will.

"I don't want to hear it. Get out."

Cannon's mouth clamps shut. "If that's what you want." The words are spoken low from between gritted teeth.

Creighton nods, and Cannon turns to head for the door. He pauses before he leaves the room. "Don't be as shortsighted as your brother."

Right then, I know he's aware of what Cav did to protect me. He probably relayed the information. My mind races with the possibilities.

What the hell am I going to do now?

We all hear the door shut, and Creighton looks like he's going to crack molars with how hard his jaw is clenched. Holly, who had already dropped her pen, crosses the room to wrap her arms around him. "I'm so sorry."

Clutching my bag tighter to my side, I head for the door. "I'm going to go work this out. I'm sorry too, Crey. I wish . . ."

I want to say I wish I'd never met Cav, but I can't make the words come out. Because they're not true. Because I love him.

But can I forgive him?

CHAPTER
THIRTY-NINE

Cav

I've searched the city for her. Every place I think she might go. I don't even know why I thought she might come here, but I got a ticket before they closed and rode the elevator up.

The Top of the Rock.

The place she waited for me for hours before giving up on me showing. What she doesn't know is that I did come. I came to tell her good-bye, but I couldn't say the words to her face. I was a coward.

I can still picture her . . .

The skirt of Greer's black dress flapped in the wind. It was May, but still cold. She'd asked to meet me here, and I knew she wanted to use tonight to forget everything that had happened these last few days.

She stared out over the city, the city she might as well be a princess of. I knew before that I had no business being part of her life, other than as the man who watched over her and kept her out of harm's way. Somehow, in those long hours of keeping watch, I felt like I knew her. But I was wrong. I didn't know Greer until the day she sat down at my table and threw my world off-balance. I didn't fall in love with her until she stole my heart out from under my guard.

I would lie, cheat, and kill for this woman. And I had. I would do anything to protect her.

Even cut myself out of her life.

My meeting with Dom this afternoon had sealed it. I was banished from the family for carrying out a hit without sanction. He gave me a deadline—be out of the city by midnight. As much as I wanted to ask Greer to run with me, I couldn't do it. The future ahead of her was too bright for her to be dragged down into my mess of a life. But somehow, I would become a better man for her. One that would deserve her. I would find a way.

I knew tonight was good-bye. I also knew if I stood in front of her, I wouldn't be able to get the words out. I knew from watching her that she'd reserved a room at a hotel a few blocks away. She was a woman on a mission—she wanted to erase her sorrow with passion.

On any other day, I would have let her use me any way she needed, but I had blood on my hands, and I couldn't taint her with that.

So, tonight I was proving I was a better man than I'd thought. I was letting her go.

"Good-bye, Greer."

My words were lost on the wind, and she didn't turn around until I was already out of sight.

Today I'm standing in the same place, staring at the same woman, but my intent is completely different. I'm not leaving without her. She's mine, and I'll fight heaven and hell to keep her. The sins of the past may not stay buried where they belong, but I refuse to let them rule our future.

No man will ever love her as much as I do.

"Greer." I say her name but it's lost on the wind, just like my good-bye three years ago.

I cross the roof, the noise of the city dying away as my focus narrows to her. She turns, pushes off the railing, and freezes when she sees me. Her dark eyes go wide as I stride toward her, stopping a foot away.

"What are you—"

I wrap my arms around her and haul her against me. "I can't let you go this time."

She tugs her arms free from where they're trapped between us, and for the length of a heartbeat, I fear she's going to push me away.

But she doesn't.

She wraps them around my neck and clings to me.

"I can't let you go either. Last time I didn't have a choice, but this time I do. I love you. I don't care what you did, because I know you did it for me."

Thank fuck.

I crush my mouth against hers, taking her lips, and Greer's fingers curl around my nape, pulling me closer. For long moments, there's nothing and no one but us.

Until we hear the clapping.

I grudgingly release Greer, lowering her to her feet as I scan the crowd of onlookers that has formed. There are only a dozen or so, but their phones are out, and I know this is going to be all over YouTube within minutes.

"Are you rehearsing for a movie? Because I want to see that one," a lady calls out.

Greer presses her face into my chest, but her laugh sneaks up between us. "If they only knew," she whispered. "If they only knew."

I look down as she releases her grip on me. "You ready to go home, baby?"

"Where's home, exactly?"

It's just one more thing we need to work out . . . but I go with my gut.

"The Hollywood Hills. I think you were born to be a California girl."

Greer slips her hand into mine. "Then take me home, Cav."

EPILOGUE

Greer

A year later

I'm just leaving Starbucks, iced coffee in hand, when a woman asks me, "So, are you going to say yes?"

It's Hollywood. I've gotten used to being recognized, but people mostly leave me alone.

"Excuse me?" I pause at her table.

"Are you going to say yes?" This time she holds up her iPad, and I see the text of an ad on a popular gossip site.

"May I?" I ask before snatching it out of her hands when she nods. The ad was posted only minutes ago.

> *Desperately seeking gorgeous, caring, perfect woman with a huge heart to make an honest man out of me and give Hollywood a happily-ever-after like it has never seen before.*
>
> *I've got a big . . . ring, just sayin'.*
>
> *GREER KARAS—WILL YOU MARRY ME?*

He didn't. *He did.*

That man. *That man.*

I hand her back the iPad. The grin on my face can't be wiped off to save my life. Some things are permanent. Apparently, like me and Cav.

"I think I owe him the answer first, don't you?"

Her smile and shrug are well meaning, and she holds out a Sharpie and a napkin. "Could I have your autograph?"

Shifting my purse, I set my iced coffee down and sign my name, and then grab another napkin and quickly draw something for myself before folding it up and sliding it in my purse.

When I moved in with Cav a year ago, I didn't know what I wanted to do with my life. Never in a million years did I expect to be standing on the red carpet of a movie I was in, with Cav accompanying *me* to the premiere.

He asked me to help him run lines one night, and I got into it so much that he started bugging me to talk to his agent about auditioning for a role. I scoffed at the idea. *Scoffed.* Greer Karas was no actress.

But I was wrong.

I might not be starring in any big movies like Cav, but I'm having more fun with work than I ever thought possible.

And now it's time to get home and talk to that man of mine.

Cav

I think I'm hearing things when the knock comes at the door. I've been waiting for a frigging hour for Greer to see the ad and come home.

No one knocks on our front door because of the gate

. . .

I grab the box from the counter, hop off my stool, and slide across the wood floor in my hurry to get to the foyer. Six feet from the door, I slow.

This is it. The only time I'm ever going to ask a woman to marry me—well, other than in the ad I posted this afternoon.

Closing the remaining distance to the door, I unlock it and pull it open.

Greer stands there, holding a heart drawn on a napkin in black marker. "It's not huge, but it's the best I could manage under the circumstances."

"I love you, Greer." The feeling hasn't dimmed in the time we've spent together, only grown. "I love you so damn much." I drop to a knee. "I've been thinking about this for four years. What I would do. What I would need to say to convince you to say yes."

It's not smooth or polished, but the words are raw honesty.

"All you had to say is exactly what you did. I love you too, so much that sometimes I feel like there's nothing else holding the pieces of me together. This has been yours since before I even realized you stole it." She holds out the napkin.

I lift the box I'm holding. "I think this is a fair trade."

Flipping the top open, I wait for her reaction. It *is* big, but it's not a diamond. It's tanzanite, which I read is a thousand times rarer than diamonds. It seems perfectly fitting for the most amazing woman I've ever met.

Greer's eyes go wide when she sees the brilliant blue stone surrounded by diamonds.

"How long have you had that?"

It's not a question I was expecting, but I tell her the truth. I always tell Greer the truth.

"Eleven months."

"Are you serious?"

"I bought it after you moved in. In case you were wondering, I never planned to let you leave."

"Why did you wait so damn long?"

"Your brother. Jerk-off wouldn't give his blessing until he saw I could make you happy for a year."

As much as it pisses me off, I understand his protectiveness. I've won his respect—grudgingly.

"You actually waited? For Crey's blessing?" Greer's tone is incredulous.

"He's family. I wasn't going to piss him off for the rest of our lives. He matters to you, Greer. So that means he matters to me."

"I love you. You didn't need his blessing—I never would've cared."

Even though Greer says that, I know it's important to her. Greer's uncle's death was ruled to be natural causes until her aunt's body was found a week later at the family house in the Hamptons with a suicide note admitting to poisoning her husband "like he'd poisoned everything else in his life." The autopsy techs still haven't figured out what kind of poison Greer's aunt used or whether she'd been mentally unstable when she'd done it, but the case is considered closed.

In that same week, Stephen Cardelli was found dead in the showers at Rikers for no apparent reason. Dom swore he knew nothing about it, and I hadn't pushed it.

Regardless, that means the last remaining family Greer has is her brother. My brother.

Creighton and I had words about that too. Over a beer. Like actual brothers. We'll never be as close as he and Greer are, but he doesn't want me on the opposite side of the country from his sister anymore.

Last night, I got an e-mail from him.

Better make an honest woman out of my sister pretty fucking soon. No man will ever be good enough for her, but you're damn close.

Today is exactly one year from the day I stood at Greer's door to answer her ad. It seemed the perfect time to do what I wish I could have done years ago.

"So, is that a yes?" I ask, still kneeling at her feet.

"That's a *hell yes.*" Greer laughs and holds out her hand.

I breathe a sigh of relief and slip the ring onto her finger before I rise.

Greer bites her lip, staring down at the ring before looking back up at me. "So, are you going to let me in?"

Backing into the house, I move so Greer can shut the

door behind us. She wraps her hands around my shoulders and turns me so my back presses against it.

"If we're going to stick to the script . . . I think we both know what happens next," she whispers.

"Damn right, we do."

The End

You know you don't want to miss what's coming next for the Dirty series! Click here to sign up for my newsletter, and never miss another announcement about upcoming projects, new releases, sales, exclusive excerpts, and giveaways.

I'd love to hear what you thought about Greer and Cav's story. If you have a few moments to leave a review, I'd be incredibly grateful. Send me a link at meghanmarchbooks@gmail.com, and I'll thank you with a personal note.

ACKNOWLEDGMENTS

Special thanks goes out to:

To every reader and blogger who picked up this duet—thank you for following me on Greer and Cav's journey. This story has been in my head for over a year, impatiently waiting its turn to be written. I hope you're enjoying the Dirty world, because I'm not ready to leave it yet. I've fallen in love with these characters, so I think I'm going to stay a little while longer.

To the amazing members of Meghan March's Runaway Readers—you've made our group my most favorite place on the Internet, and I can't thank you enough for your unending support. I hope I get to meet and hug you all in person.

To my JJL Crew—I love you all so fucking much. You're my soul sisters.

Angela Smith of Grey Ghost Author Services, LLC, my amazing PA and best friend. Can you believe how far we've come? I wouldn't know what to do without you in my life. I never want to find out.

Angela Marshall Smith and Pam Berehulke, editors extraordinaire, for once again helping me deliver an amazing story.

Danielle Sanchez and the Inkslinger PR team, best-in-class publicists, for handling this release with professionalism and style.

Natasha Gentile and Jamie Lynn, my fabulous beta readers, for riding this crazy train without question and not chasing me down with pitchforks when I hadn't finished *Dirty Love* when you read *Dirty Girl*.

Hang Le, for once again creating a fabulous cover—I love it so much.

Darren Birks, for capturing the perfect cover images.

Stacey Blake of Champagne Formats, for the gorgeous interior design and amazingly quick turnaround.

My family, for their constant support of my big dreams. I love you all.

Also by Meghan March

Author's Note

I'd love to hear from you. Connect with me at:

UNAPOLOGETICALLY SEXY ROMANCE

Website: www.meghanmarch.com

Facebook: www.facebook.com/MeghanMarchAuthor

Twitter: www.twitter.com/meghan_march

Instagram: www.instagram.com/meghanmarch

ABOUT THE AUTHOR

Meghan March has been known to wear camo face paint and tromp around in the woods wearing mud-covered boots, all while sporting a perfect manicure. She's also impulsive, easily entertained, and absolutely unapologetic about the fact that she loves to read and write smut.

Her past lives include slinging auto parts, selling lingerie, making custom jewelry, and practicing corporate law. Writing books about dirty-talking alpha males and the strong, sassy women who bring them to their knees is by far the most fabulous job she's ever had.

She loves hearing from her readers at:

meghanmarchbooks@gmail.com

Made in the USA
Lexington, KY
25 April 2017